T0007760

Published by Semiotext(e)
PO BOX 629, South Pasadena, CA 91031
www.semiotexte.com

Cover Art: Annette Messager, "Sleeping Purple Passion," 2018. © 2023 Artists Rights Society (ARS), New York / ADAGP, Paris

Cover Design: Dorothée Perret
Layout: Hedi El Kholti
ISBN: 978-1-63590-177-1

Distributed by the MIT Press, Cambridge, MA.
Printed and bound in the United States of America.

Sleepless

A Memoir of Insomnia

Marie Darrieussecq

Translated by Penny Hueston

semiotext(e)

Contents

Prologue

I lost sleep. I retraced my steps but sleep wasn't following me. It had broken free and I was wandering through the night without it.

What wild beast has devoured my sleep? I'm hunting it down in the forest. I've got leads. The killer left clues.

I used to be able to sleep. I thought I had a grip on my sleep. I thought it followed me like my shadow—that it was my shadow. Sleep, I thought, is the other half of us, our safe haven, our escape route. It is us, in our absence.

Not sleeping: wandering around without a shadow.

In January 2017, I began writing a column on insomnia for a weekly magazine. I even sent the publisher a plan for umpteen columns on the subject: one of the editors there jokingly called it "the thousand and one nights of insomnia." In the end I stitched together a column a month over two years, like a Fair Isle knitting pattern, which I shortened, lengthened, and often improvised. For this book I went back to the beginning. The beginning of no-sleep. In my columns I had tried to weave my insomnia into what was going on in the news, but insomnia has its own news cycle. It occurs absolutely in the present. Only sleepers are kept awake by what happened yesterday or what will happen tomorrow. In "the brutality of no-sleep," said Marguerite Duras, insomnia has no "theme."[1] Nothing disrupts the insomniac. No event. No spark of daylight illuminates the insomniac's relationship with the night. Nothing prevents the insomniac from not sleeping.

I've got plenty to read during my unending insomnia. Every book I open talks about insomnia. Gide! Pavese! Plath! Sontag! Kafka! Dostoevsky! Darwish! Murakami! Césaire! Borges![2] U Tam'si![3] And so many other champions of fatigue. On every continent, that's all literature talks about. As if writing was not-sleeping. As if *literature* was an anagram of *lie in torture, literal tear, little terror* …

In literature, the patron saint of insomnia is Kafka. If I could pray, I'd pray to Kafka; his whole oeuvre is one long night of insomnia haunted by ghosts: "Dread of night. Dread of not-night."[4] The proprietor of insomnia is the philosopher Cioran: "Those who have not personally endured this tragedy will not have the slightest understanding of it. Insomnia is the most profound experience one can have in life."[5] And the champion of insomnia is Proust, whose work opens with literature's most famous failed bedtime: "For a long time I would go to bed early. Sometimes, the candle barely out, my eyes closed so quickly that I did not have time to tell myself: 'I'm falling asleep.' And half an hour later the thought that it was time to look for sleep would awaken me."[6]

And yet surely it doesn't just affect writers? In his story "A Clean, Well-Lighted Place," Hemingway contrasts the waiter who is in a hurry to get home to bed with the other waiter, still dawdling beneath the electric light, polishing the counter in the café. "He would lie in bed and finally, towards dawn, he would fall asleep. After all, he says to himself, it's probably only insomnia. Many must have it."[7]

I'm enthralled when I hear accounts from sleepers. *How do you sleep?* becomes my *How do you do?* One morning in Montreal, wiped out by jetlag, I met my publisher Paul Otchakovsky-Laurens, who was bright-eyed and bushy-tailed, at the stand at the book fair. He was marveling at the fresh snow, which he had photographed at five in the morning for his wife in Paris. "So you didn't sleep?" I asked him, somewhat hopefully. He'd woken, glimpsed the beauty of the snowflakes, and then gone straight back to sleep. "When it comes to sleep," he told me, "I've got the knack."

What exactly does this "knack" consist of?

Hidden in our attics, crouching beneath our mattresses, sliding between the joists of time, where does insomnia come from? From ghosts? From the brain? From a troubled soul? From the world?

I had to stop. I had to lay my insomnia to rest. Rake over it one last time and then *poof*, perhaps I'd be able to sleep. This book is the result of twenty years of panic, and of journeys through books and through my nights.

I

The Deep Sleep in My Skull

I can't sleep. I can't sleep. I can't sleep.
Vast sleepiness throughout my body and mind,
* covering my eyes, all through my soul!*
The only thing not sleeping is my inability to sleep!
                                      —Fernando Pessoa[1]

To Sleep or Not to Sleep

The world is divided into those who can sleep and those who can't.

The prophet Jonah is the patron saint of good sleepers. Disobeying God did not prevent him from sleeping right through the storm, which was God's anger.

> Then the mariners were afraid, and cried every man unto his god, and cast forth the wares that were in the ship into the sea, to lighten it of them. But Jonah was gone down into the sides of the ship; and he lay, and was fast asleep. So the shipmaster came to him, and said unto him, "What meanest thou, O sleeper? Arise, call upon thy God."[2]

Isn't it his extraordinary ability to sleep that marks Jonah out as different? An argument blows up, he is thrown into the ocean, and, *gulp*, the whale swallows him. Inside the whale's belly for three days, Jonah has time to get dry and to deliberate. But who's to say that, for those three nights, he's not asleep?

When it comes to sleep and anxiety, we are not equal.

"I want to write these lines before I fall asleep. Because I know I'm going to fall asleep despite everything that has happened," writes Hélène Berr, even though her father has just been deported and she has been wearing the yellow star for a month. It's 11:15 p.m. on Thursday, July 2, 1942.[3]

Winston Churchill had a bed in his office. He claimed that his afternoon naps "helped win the war." No one was allowed to wake him "unless the British Isles were being invaded."

As for President Obama, he lamented that he had to limit his sleep to six hours a night. His colleagues were allowed to wake him "only if there was a major crisis," an instruction that left them racked with doubt.

Samuel Pepys, British member of Parliament and hyperactive chief secretary to the Admiralty, recorded in his famous diary on September 24, 1665, at the height of the Great Plague and amid a deluge of dead bodies, that he had never experienced such "happiness and pleasure" in the face of so many problems to solve. Exactly a year later, his first reaction to the Great Fire of London was to go back to sleep; his servant had to shake him to get him out of bed.

I admire such good sleepers. Masters of sleep, who know how to sleep whatever happens.

What is their secret? Do they have, as conventional wisdom would have it, *a clear conscience*? Victor Hugo said it (he said everything, just like Churchill): "A clear conscience is worth more than a prosperous life. I prefer a good sleep to a good bed." Footballers are particularly fond of this platitude. When criticized for his tactics, Míchel, manager of the Marseille football club OM, told *Goal* magazine on January 19, 2016: "I sleep very well, I have a clear conscience." The Spanish footballer Sergio Ramos, criticized for his playing style, gave a similar response on France Inter on June 15, 2018: "Honestly, I sleep very well at night. I have a clear conscience." After his run-in with coach Raymond Domenech, the French footballer Nicolas Anelka announced to the *Journal du Dimanche* on June 9, 2018: "When you tell the truth you sleep well. And I sleep very well."

What, then, is the insomniac hiding? What unmentionable torment haunts her nights? To sleep poorly is poorly regarded. "Luck comes to us while we sleep," says Vautrin to Rastignac in Balzac's *Father Goriot*.[4] And in Kafka's *The Castle* all the bigwigs go to sleep well fed and content. The only recourse left to the sleep-deprived, insulted even in their despair, is for them to believe that they are ennobled by their wakefulness. Their insomnia would then accommodate the cause of the world's tribulations. The famous "sleep of the just" would then become the sleep of the forgetful. "Jesus will be in agony until the end of the world. There must be no sleeping during that time"—one of Pascal's "thoughts," and not a very comforting one.[5] It would be altruistic, even charitable, not to sleep: "In Mali, if you have eaten and your neighbor hasn't, you cannot sleep peacefully," says Mouhamadou Camara, executive secretary of the High Council for Malians in the diaspora.[6] A terse line from Pierre Reverdy in 1916: "Sleeping serenely is no longer possible once you have opened your eyes."[7] So too bad for those who sleep well, especially in the middle of a war. And Violette Leduc agrees in *I Hate People Who Sleep*: "A dead person left in a bedroom is more benevolent than a sleeping person."[8]

The insomniac is noble; only idiots sleep. "He scarcely knows that he is asleep," says Proust of "a man who falls straight into bed night after night."[9] And there are no two ways about it for Marguerite Duras: "I think insomnia is a path towards what I would call a higher intelligence."[10] The same idea is in the *Matrix* movies: those who sleep miss out; only those who are wide awake, the heroes, can see the famous matrix, and then they're struck by insomnia in *The Matrix Reloaded*—in short, driven to despair, reduced to idiocy by exhaustion. "The last refuge of the insomniac is a sense of superiority to the sleeping world."[11] So said Leonard Cohen, and he knew all about sleepless nights.

So insomnia is classier than sleep. Only the tragic hero is an insomniac, according to Barthes.[12] Attendants hear out the story of the kings' misfortunes, then go off and have a nap.

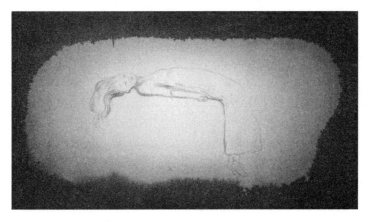

Françoise Pétrovitch, *Étendu* (Stretched out), 2016

"Thrice have the shades of night obscured the heav'ns / Since sleep has enter'd thro' your eyes," says Oenone anxiously to Phaedra, in Jean Racine's play.[13] But who is going to worry about Oenone's sleepless nights? Don Quixote is awake while Sancho Panza snoozes. For the miners in Zola's *Germinal*, "When Sunday came one slept from weariness," but it only takes the wind to keep the delicate Cécile awake.[14]

Since sleeping is an urge almost as vulgar as defecating, it is the will of the aristocrats to usurp the privilege of staying wide awake. "One does not sleep when one has such a brain [as myself]," reflects Conte Mosca in *The Charterhouse of Parma*.[15] And, in Balzac's world, aristocratic women at best only rest, while ordinary women collapse with fatigue: "Madame Camusot entered the bedroom of the beautiful Diane de Maufrigneuse, who, though she had gone to bed at one o'clock in the morning, was still not asleep at nine."[16]

And do poets snore? Insomnia and writing both thrive on the fantasy of the chosen. Victor Hugo slept badly: there's nothing more glamorous than the battle of *Hernani* to bring on insomnia.[17] But Jean Valjean from *Les Misérables* also falls victim to insomnia, which bestows visionary powers on him, even in the darkness of the sewers, and manifests as a throbbing migraine from which he emerges as a full-fledged person. For Valjean, insomnia is his very conscience. It ennobles the former convict.

Of course, you don't have to be a convict to work out that sleep is more difficult if you're sentenced to hard labor rather than staying at Diane de Maufrigneuse's place in *The Human Comedy*. And we all know that form of insomnia brought on by stress or alcohol abuse, an early train to catch that keeps us wired, a coffee drunk too late in the day that leaves us agitated … But "real" insomnia does not care in the slightest about objective causes, and it crosses all social classes. "One is vigilant when there is nothing more to be vigilant about and despite the absence of any reason to be vigilant," wrote Emmanuel Levinas, for whom insomnia belongs in the realm of metaphysics.[18] This random insomnia moves through our lives with the indifference of a despot sentencing us: you will not sleep.

Life's Worries That Continue during the Night

Marguerite Duras also distinguished between insomnia that was "metaphysical, without any reason," and occasional bouts of insomnia, "life's worries that continue during the night."[19] "I didn't sleep all night," sleepers say to insomniacs, who feel like replying that they *haven't slept all their life.*

Insomnia can begin like a quick jig, occasional worries, troubling but fleeting, and then end up dancing its way into something serious. "I didn't sleep a wink all night thinking about it," said Léa Salamé, a well-known French radio and television commentator, who had to write an article for the first time in her life in 2016. "I couldn't sleep all night I was so disappointed," said Inès, when she was eliminated from *Koh-Lanta*, the French reality show based on *Survivor*. Likewise Huw, another unhappy contestant on the same show: "I couldn't sleep all night, I rehashed it the whole night long, I was so incredibly annoyed." Madame de Sévigné, after the departure of her daughter for Provence on the morning of February 6, 1671: "Black awakenings during the night, and in the morning I was not a step nearer finding rest for my soul."[20] And the resident of Toulouse who won €32 million in the EuroMillions lottery on May 28, 2019, couldn't sleep that night and ended up hiding his winning ticket in the pocket of a shirt hanging in his wardrobe.

The sorrows of the young Esther, by Riad Sattouf

It was the same thing for Sara Forestier after the 2020 César Awards ceremony in which Roman Polanski won Best Director: "I should have left the room. We should all have left the room. I couldn't sleep all night."[21]

Likewise, Ai Fen, chief physician of a private clinic near the Wuhan market, who already understood on January 1, 2020, that the coronavirus was spreading between humans. At 11:46 p.m. she received this message from the "director of the Central Commission for Discipline Inspection at the hospital: *Come and see me tomorrow.* She didn't sleep all night."[22]

After his meeting with Trump, James Comey, sacked head of the FBI, was awake at night with anxiety and decided in bed to leak their conversation. In fact, after the election of

Trump, the American media identified a new phenomenon, Trump-induced insomnia, which was unfortunately persistent, just like PBI, post-Brexit insomnia, which afflicted a number of worried British people.[23]

And Aegisthus can't sleep at the thought of Orestes's return—his insomnia sometimes gleaming like a dagger. But it's not the case for Electra; insomnia is her destiny: "Allow those eyes overcome by insomnia to be delivered into sleep!" pleads Orestes, her brother and fellow assassin.[24] But will the sparkling Electra ever sleep, she of the name filled with lightning and fury?

Eyelids Cut Off

The Roman consul Marcus Atilius Regulus died of insomnia 2,200 years ago. His is the oldest recorded case of insomnia. Defeated at Carthage by Xanthippus's army of elephants, he was condemned to have his eyelids cut off. And then, as if that wasn't enough, he was encased in a chest lined with spikes and forced to look at the sun. A myth as genuine as glory, as reliable as Roman virtue. In Turner's painting you can't see the tortured consul; you are inside his subjective, cauterized vision. The sun is a sabre cleaving the space in two. Incandescent haze. The eyes of Regulus are molten.[25]

Turner, *Regulus*, 1828 (Tate, London). The town is split on either side of what could be a canal of tears.

Sleep-deprivation torture is still practiced in China, in Guantanamo, in Saudi Arabia, in Morocco.[26] Iratxe Sorzabal, a member of the Basque-nationalist movement ETA, recalls being held in custody for five days in 2001 inside a high-security wing of a Spanish police station: "If I testified in the way they wanted me to, they would let me sleep."[27] In her case there was no need for shackles, a chest lined with spikes, or removal of the eyelids: she endured constant light, deafening music, 24/7 surveillance, being forced to stand, or balance on one foot, or even lie down, because the torture was not about position but about insomnia itself. In a report from Amnesty International denouncing "clean, contactless" torture, I read how insomnia by coercion makes one "more sensitive to the cold, to heat, to pain, makes the eyes and limbs swell, and upsets the digestive system." All you need is a few days of this unbearable experience for prisoners to blurt out whatever you want them to and then sink into a state of "pathological submission." Sleep as a means of escape is no longer possible. The here and now is unremitting—torture that leads to madness.

On Devil's Island, Alfred Dreyfus kept a prison diary about his enforced wakefulness. "The guards changed shift every two hours; they were under instruction not to take their eyes off me, day and night. In order to execute the latter part of their duty, the cell was illuminated all night." Kept under constant surveillance, shackled nightly, he was completely unable to sleep: "I know of no worse torture, I certainly know of no worse torture than lying on a bed without sleeping." Even though there was a view of the sea from his cell, it had been blocked off by a fence. The writing in his diary is gradually replaced by multiplying variations of the same doodle.[28]

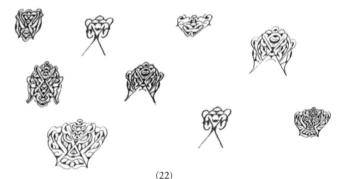

He was a prisoner for four years; "that is, one thousand five hundred days and as many nights." Alfred Dreyfus, *Cahiers de Île du diable* (Notebooks from Devil's Island), 1989.

Four O'clock or Whatever Time in the Morning

"Agonies in bed towards morning. Saw only solution in jumping out of the window." Kafka, August 15, 1913.[29]

"People commit suicide because they can't sleep," stated Cioran.[30] His first published work, a book of essays written when he was twenty-two, was entitled *On the Heights of Despair*, no less. Insomnia and fascism were the two demons that had a firm hold on the young Cioran. In Sibiu, Transylvania, in 1933, he was wandering through the fog of the Romanian night, among the lurking vampires. Forty-five years later, in the preface to a new edition of the book, not much has changed: "The crucial circumstance, the overriding disaster, is uninterrupted sleeplessness, that unending void.... Anything is preferable to permanent wakefulness, to that criminal absence of forgetfulness." In this "vertiginous lucidity," having a break from oneself, even for a few hours, is an impossible dream.[31] "Shocking night. At four in the morning I was more awake than in broad daylight. Thought about Celan. It must have been on a night like this when he suddenly decided to end it."[32]

Two o'clock, three o'clock, four o'clock. Insomnia without end.

On the morning of February 1, 1980, Alix Cléo Roubaud, twenty-eight years old, wrote: "The horror arrives in the morning / It doesn't come from the morning itself but from the night and it makes itself felt when it outlives the night / when in the morning the world has kept its night-face." And she adds, in smaller script: "Oh, my God, what am I doing here at seven o'clock in the morning, sleepless night, no cigarettes, all smoked, paper all around."[33]

The mornings after the nights when one has not slept are dead mornings. Get up; look as if you're getting up. Insomnia never leaves you, it is there during the day, it clings to you. A night without sleep extends into a day without sleep. Nothing time that consumes you nonetheless.

Incapable of doing anything whatsoever. Incapable of doing anything. Incapable of being here. "In a way, my skeleton was all that was holding me together," wrote Alix Cléo Roubaud. The next minute is impossible to live, impossible to see coming, the next minute is the last thing I want.

Annette Messager, *Petite dance du matin* (Little Morning Dance), April 2020

I can't sleep; I can't read when I lie awake at night,
I can't write when I lie awake at night,
I can't think when I lie awake at night—
My God, I can't even dream when I lie awake at night!
(Pessoa)[34]

At 4:44 a.m. it's too early to get up and too late to start living ... *Too late to end it now / Too early to start again*, sings Charlotte Gainsbourg in "5:55."[35] The Germans call it *schnapps o'clock*. When you see double and triple. In the film *The Amityville Horror*, the devil knocks on the door at 3:33 a.m. During insomnia, the witching hour blinks on and off. The Beast has jammed the clocks and the night promises no dawn. For Sarah Kane, it is 4:48 a.m., the cruelest time of insomnia, the time to end things.[36] It's 5:05 a.m. when the narrator turns on the gas in Violette Leduc's *Ravages*.[37]

Marguerite Duras, 1985: "During serious bouts of insomnia, one says to oneself, 'If I died this instant, what a relief that would be.'" She points out that the worst time "is around three or four in the morning."[38] In his detached style, Christian Oster writes: "To die at four in the morning, in the discomfort of insomnia, constitutes a form of temptation, the hope of bailing out and coming to terms with silence. Anyway, that's what it's like for me. There are people who cope better with those moments, at least I think so, in the absence of a survey on the subject; I'm only speaking for those in my camp; there's no point in trying to persuade the others if they're happy to wake at four in the morning, alone and a nervous wreck."[39]

There's no end to this four-in-the-morning literature, just as midnight will always strike and there will always be the devil in the bottle. F. Scott Fitzgerald knew all about it: "What if this night prefigured the night after death.... I am a ghost now as the clock strikes four."[40]

And then there's this doggerel from Victor Hugo, who was short on sleep and sometimes wrote too much:

> But to wake up and ponder in the deep
> Of night, dreary, alone, when all things are asleep
> Mysterious! …
> Still imprisoned by Morpheus. Leave me alone!
> Master, what do you want? Do show me some
> courtesy!
> A most pigheaded demon you must be
> To come and wake me when all things are still!
> Look, I'll open an eye now—will
> That please you? Not one chink of light from the
> windowsill![41]

And when Okonkwo, the hero of Chinua Achebe's *Things Fall Apart*, drags himself out of bed after a night of no sleep, he feels "like a drunken giant walking with the limbs of a mosquito."[42] He doesn't mention the time because we are in a world without clocks, but it is the dead of night in Lower Niger, colonized by the British.

"It was four-thirty by the time they got to the Forensic Institute."[43] In book after book, it's always that time in the morning for Inspector Maigret and his assistant. It was after a trip to Simenon's birthplace in the fair city of Liège, where I didn't sleep a wink, that I set about reading all Simenon's books, in search of his all-nighters. A psycho-analyst friend then pointed out to me that *Simenon* is, apart from a missing *i*, an anagram of *insomnie*.

I stopped collecting four-in-the-morning literature.

II

Searching for So Long

My whole life long, I never searched for anything
as much as I searched for sleep.
— Tezer Özlü[1]

Sleep, sleep, how?

The passageway is shut. The door has disappeared. The wall is smooth. Sleep is known only by name, like a myth, like a phantom.

How, how? What does one do in order to sleep? That's all, sleep. Sleep—with oneself, by oneself. Find sleep within oneself.

Or prick one's finger on a spindle and fall asleep like Sleeping Beauty.

There are sleep champions. They rest their head on the pillow and off they glide, hurtling down the slope. The wave curls. The sky opens up. Oceanic sleep. Their arms supported by atoms alone. With crazy ease, with an astounding knowledge of abysses, they never fall. But we insomniacs plummet into horrendous ravines and the bags under our eyes are bruise colored.

Sleep is a sport of gliding. While in a sanatorium in the Tatra Mountains in 1921, as he watched some skiers, Kafka described it in a letter to Max Brod: "For them there were no slopes, no ditches, no embankments; they glided over the terrain like your pen over paper.... It was like a dream, like the way a healthy man glides from waking into sleep."[2] How? How does one launch oneself? *Launch* is a skiing term: to initiate a turn, "gambol among avalanches" in Rimbaud's words.[3] Ah, to glide into a hypnagogic state, to witness one's consciousness morph into dream images, smoothly linked ... And everything would become white, white as snow, white as a sheet, white as a sleeping pill.

Without sleeping pills, I can't do it.

Sleeping Pills

I've been running on barbiturates for almost thirty years. I savor soporifics, I booze on benzodiazepines, I stagnate on sedatives, I'm hypnotic with narcotics.

I remember the first time I took one, the night before an exam, in 1990. A quarter of a Lexomil, given to me by a girlfriend. I loved it. The wave of relaxation. The guarantee of sleep on its way. You head out on the frozen lake; the ice doesn't give way. Leisurely, you reach the opposite bank. No waking up in the frozen water. All these years, I've been juggling little white pills. I've tried various brands and experienced a range of enjoyment. Imovane, Atarax, Temesta, Donormyl are my usuals. Noctran was withdrawn from the market a while ago, and as of April 10, 2017, Stilnox is, alas, only available in France via a doctor's validated prescription. When I tried cannabis essence, I felt wasted all day.

Sometimes all I need is to *have the packet*. I gaze at it. I know it's there. Proust recommends this method: "It's a mistake to resign yourself to insomnia.... I consulted Brissaud, an admirable man, with vast intelligence, but a poor physician, who thought (I'm not exaggerating) that one should live on Trional.... If you had, for example, taken the barbiturate one or two times and slept, you would have your pills on your bedside table and, instead of swallowing them (according to the Brissaud method), you would know they were there ... that sense of security would be enough to allow you to sleep."[4]

Real sleeping pills, ones that work, are hard to obtain without a prescription. It means having a doctor, going through the ritual of seducing the doctor, and sometimes the pharmacist; it means having connections, conniving in

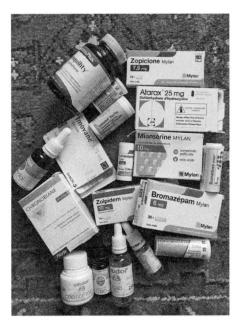

My stash. Enough to take care of the problem once and for all.

some way. Whether you like it or not, you're engaged in a relationship, you stick with the prescriber who comes up with the goods, you move on from the schmucks. In the powerful opening scene of Mike Leigh's 2010 film *Another Year*, an exhausted female worker (played by Imelda Staunton) who wants nothing more than to sleep has to contend with a female psychologist who wants nothing more than to treat her; the sleepless woman ends up begging for a prescription for sleeping pills, while the therapist confuses consultation and domination.

"The progress of insomnia is remarkable, and keeps pace with all other progress. How many people in the world now sleep a synthetic sleep only, and get their supply of oblivion from the skilled industry of organic chemistry!"[5] You are so right, Valéry, and this progress is only getting worse, with more and more products, and ever-increasing profits for pharmaceutical companies. And just as you can choose beer rather than wine, or rum rather than whisky, every sleeping tablet has its frequency and dosage, directions for use, its side effects, its attendant dreams, its downward spiral, its addiction, its affliction. Combined with alcohol, their effect is enhanced. It's best to do without them. I've tried to.

When I don't take them, I don't sleep. And when I don't sleep, I want to die, so I read, or I try to read. In Ottessa Moshfegh's novel *My Year of Rest and Relaxation*, the narrator takes, in no particular order and often at the same time, Sofolton, Infermiterol, Pronosticrone, Ambien (Stilnox), Rozerem, Seconal, Neuroproxine, Librium, meprobamate, ethchlorvynol, quetiapine, trazodone, Ris-perdal, Maxiphenphen, Valdignore, Silencior, Rohypnol, Temesta, Xanax, Valium, Nembutal, Dimetapp, Benadryl, melatonin, Lunesta, temazepam, oxycodone, haloperidol, Klonopin, Zyprexa … I made a note of the drugs as I read the novel; not all of them exist, or at least not in Europe, or not under these names. "I even made myself a cup of chamomile tea," the narrator adds. She is funny. On the verge of a somnambulic coma—sometimes waking up covered in scum, her clothes torn—she ends up asking a friend to lock her in her apartment. "I might jump out the window, I thought, if I couldn't sleep."[6] This shuffling on the edge of the abyss describes, with black humor, a particular condition of American culture and of American women, and comes to an end with a brutal awakening on September 11, 2001.

So now I only read to keep company with fellow addicts of sleeping pills. In *Destroy, She Said* by Marguerite Duras, two insomniac men are fascinated by a woman knocked out by "white tablets," who sleeps in order to survive the death of her child. In the play *The Bitter Tears of Petra von Kant*, Petra von Kant soliloquizes: "I love you so much, Mother! You take some tablets, drop them in water, swallow them … and sleep. It's so good to sleep. I haven't slept for so long. I want to sleep. A long, long sleep."[7] And in *A Sorrow Beyond Dreams: A Life Story*, Peter Handke recounts his mother's experiences: "She took sleeping pills but usually woke up soon after midnight; then she would cover her face with her pillow. She lay awake trembling until it was light, and the trembling lasted all day."[8]

When it comes to books by men, *Night Roads* by Clément Rosset and *Darkness Visible* by William Styron are two whose pale covers in their French Gallimard editions I tend to confuse—along with their similar subtitles, *Clinical Episodes* and *A Memoir of Madness*. They are both accounts of chronic depression by two representatives of the traditional patriarchy, one a fifty-one-year-old Frenchman, the other a sixty-year-old American, each of them addicted to sleeping pills and antidepressants (and, in Styron's case, to alcohol).

Continuing our world tour, Sadegh Hedayat, an Iranian Comte de Lautréamont who took his own life in 1950, announces on the first page of his book *The Blind Owl*: "Relief from it is to be found only in the oblivion brought about by wine and in the artificial sleep induced by opium and similar narcotics."[9] All through the twentieth century, so much of Japanese literature (Akutagawa, Kawabata, Ōe, Ogawa) is concerned with barbiturates and, by and large, suicide. In Brazil, Clarice Lispector almost died when, knocked out by sleeping pills and holding a cigarette, her mattress caught fire. In the Antilles, "Césaire was exhausted from insomnia and managed to get pharmacists on the island to hand over sleeping pills without a prescription. Pierre Aliker, his doctor, had to remove them from his pockets."[10] And back to Cioran, who wrote on April 28, 1965, "For five hours I battled to go to sleep; I even used a morphine suppository."[11]

And, of course, there's Shakespeare, whose real drama was not-sleeping. Iago warns Othello that "Not poppy nor mandragora, / Nor all the drowsy syrups of the world" will let him sleep. "Ha, ha," replies Othello.[12]

But the greatest book about sleeping pills is *In Search of Lost Time*. We know more about Proust's asthma than his insomnia, and yet the two go together—along with his anorexia.[13] Asthma prevented Proust from eating and drinking; insomnia and anorexia aggravated his asthma; he had no appetite when he was exhausted, and was incapable of sleeping when he was no longer eating. Proust's pharmacopeia included chloral hydrate (the oldest synthetic hypnotic, invented in 1832), trional (1890), veronal (1903), tetronal, sometimes heroin, Pantopon, and also opium powder in his antiasthma cigarettes. Datura, hemp, ether, belladonna, and valerian are also mentioned in *In Search of Lost Time*. The character of Bergotte, his name a combination of *iceberg* and *bergamot*, incarnates insomnia in the same way other characters in *In Search of Lost Time* incarnate vanity, duplicity, goodness, egoism. And it's no surprise that he's the writer character. Proust describes him experimenting with a new sedative: "One's heart beats as at a first assignation."[14]

Much of Proust's correspondence, as described by Dominique Mabin, is a secret conversation about the risks, benefits, and dosage of narcotics. On October 2, 1904, he writes to Princesse Hélène de Caraman-Chimay, sister of Anna de Noailles, "Such a mysterious gift, this tetronal. Through what sort of incomprehensible communion does the white wafer, which in itself seems to contain oblivion, allow me to forget my sorrows for a few hours, and leave me in the morning, on waking, more hopeful, more acquiescent? I thank you for your gift, Princess. I will owe you my sleep tonight. Until now you had given me only dreams."

Céleste Albaret, Proust's housekeeper, is a case of insomnia by solidarity. When she started work with him, she adopted a schedule to which she was already partly adjusted, as her husband Odilon was a night chauffeur. She left Monsieur Proust "just before nine in the morning," and got out of bed "about one or two in the afternoon." She looked after everything for him, beginning with his *café au lait*, two cups of an elixir made from freshly ground beans, which she would keep making for him at regular intervals, whenever he called for it. "If I dared to ask: 'But tell me, monsieur, when do you sleep?' 'I don't know, Céleste,' he would say. 'I don't know.'" The last seven weeks of his life, she didn't go to bed at all. The writer Paul Morand wondered "how she possibly kept going." "For me it was quite natural," wrote Céleste in her memoir. "He was suffering."[15]

Céleste Albaret

"I'm living in a sort of death, punctuated by brief awakenings."[16] Proust writes from within insomnia, and it is from insomnia that he elicits his writing. Insomnia is his laboratory, and it is first and foremost an experiment in time. It is the place where memory is written, the room containing the rooms of the past. Proust is the little boy sent to bed, waiting for his mother's goodnight kiss, and the famous madeleine is cooked in the oven of insomnia: dipped in tea, it has the whiff of Aunt Léonie, she who complained that she never slept. "If my aunt felt 'agitated' ... it would be my duty to shake out of the chemist's little package on to a plate the amount of lime-blossom required for infusion in boiling water."[17]

His struggle with noise was another of Proust's battles, one waged by Céleste. The earplugs he was accustomed to were not enough. When he stayed at his regular hotel in Normandy, he had to rent the rooms above and below his room. In Paris, the walls of his bedroom on boulevard Hausmann had been soundproofed with cork panels, and when he had to move out, he had them "taken down very carefully and stored in a garage so that they could be put up again when he found a suitable new flat."[18] Moving was a saga. The only possible place was a top-floor apartment with a lift. Rue de Rivoli proved to be too noisy: a train ran beneath boulevard Pereire. Finally, Proust found his sanctuary on rue Hamelin. Not exactly on the top floor, but there was only a small apartment above, occupied by a "kind lady, and M. Proust asked me to give her some money in exchange for a promise not to make any noise." Everyone, including the dentist and the harpist in the boulevard Hausmann building, made an effort "to stifle their noise and their comings and goings during the day in order not to disturb Monsieur Proust."[19]

Herbal medicines, narcotics, barbiturates, sleeping pills, hypnotic drugs, and all the rest ... The definitions of these words have evolved over time, and I'm jumbling them together here in the one pharmaceutical grab bag. In her chapter "Complications of Insomnia," Fanny Déchanet-Platz describes just how often writers, Proust above all, confuse, in their consumption and in their writing, the names of plants and products.[20] It seems to be a voluntary confusion: insomniac writers become quite simply "barbiturate addicts," and their carefully maintained muddling of drugs and sleeping pills allows them to avoid facing up to their dependence.[21]

Indeed, we find these substances throughout literature, with names like poisons or waterlilies. If Proust needs veronal to get to sleep, Nietzsche does it with chloral, Jean Genet with Nembutal, and Joan Didion with Pentothal. Like in Anne Ségalen's lyrics to Jacques Dutronc's "Lullaby":

Phenergan, Mogadon,
Tranquilizing Optalidon ...

Atarax, Immenoctal,
Olympax and Booctal ...
The garbage trucks will be coming by,
And my alarm in a quarter of an hour.[22]

And I learn that Céline, "a serious insomniac since the war ... invented Somnothryl, an anti-insomnia medication, the benefits of which he extols in an article entitled 'The Insomnia of Intellectuals,' published in *La Revue médicale de l'Est.*"[23]

One evening, when Atiq Rahimi and I were complaining to each other about how exhausted we were, I recommended he take Donormyl, available over the counter. I prescribed up to two tablets for this reluctant patient. Prudently, Atiq took half a tablet. I expected nothing less than the sort of gratitude Proust showed toward Princesse Hélène de Caraman-Chimay, but I heard nothing back from Atiq until our publisher informed me that I had almost killed him: my insomniac friend maintained that he had dragged himself around comatose for three days. When we caught up with each other again, Atiq boasted to me about products he claimed were far more reliable, some of which came from his country of birth, Afghanistan. Another friend, a Cuban, swore there was nothing like marijuana for inducing a sleep intoxicated by sweet dreams. But marijuana fumes make me feel like I'm on an unhinged merry-go-round. My dreams are far from sweet, I feel dizzy, the bed sweeps me into a vortex that I can only be dragged out of by dancing, by friends—in short, by a party, not sleep.

And the more I hear from insomniacs—that is, half the world—the better I understand how sleeping products affect every individual differently. Another insomniac friend, Nicolas Fargues, told me that he had stopped taking Donormyl a long time ago. He had become completely addicted to this antihistamine, which only delivered him a light sleep filled with fitful dreams. Nicolas ended up accepting his insomnia, living with it. He slept very little at night, allowed himself a nap on Sunday, and worked a lot. As well as writing, he was the multimedia librarian at the French Institute of Yaoundé, where he put me up while I was writing *Men*, a nocturnal novel in which there is also no sleep.

Insomniac selfie, at Nicolas's house in Yaoundé, January 2013

Overdoses

One of the dangers of sleeping pills is that they attack the short-term memory. "Chloral makes holes in my brain," Proust confided to Paul Morand. And you can die from those memory lapses: you don't remember when you took the first dose or the second. You say to yourself, *It's not possible*, not possible to *not sleep* so much. So you take more. The self-medicating insomniac is flirting with death; the tightrope walker living on a suspended sentence juggles the white tablets of his addiction.

"Sleeping is not dying," Barbara says in her song "Insomnia"; she is making it clear that, earlier in her life, when she had ended up in a coma, it was an accidental overdose, not an attempted suicide. The precise term would be an *attempted sleep*.

How many celebrities have ended up dead in the hope of sleeping? Michael Jackson (lorazepam and propofol), Prince (fentanyl), Jimi Hendrix (alcohol and nine tablets of Seconal), Judy Garland (alcohol and ten tablets of Seconal) … And then—familiar victims of the Hollywood slaughterhouse—countless young up-and-coming actors and actresses. Or twenty-eight-year-old Heath Ledger, who played the Joker in the excellent Batman film *The Dark Knight*, directed by Christopher Nolan, and who died after taking a cocktail of six different prescription sleeping tablets and antianxiety medications. Friends described him complaining often that he had trouble sleeping. "Dammit, I can't sleep," he'd say. I'm filled with a maternal urge to cradle this young Joker in my arms. There's no end of dramatic accidents stemming from insomnia—they're all there to explore in an open-pit mine on Wikipedia. Such as Anna Nicole Smith, 1993 Playmate of the Year and reality-TV star, who died "accidentally"—again, I'm quoting from an autopsy report—aged thirty-nine, from an overdose of eleven different sleeping pills, antidepressants, antihistamines, painkillers, and tranquilizers. Six months earlier, her twenty-year-old son had also died "accidentally" from a combination of two different antidepressants, along with methadone and Stilnox.

And then there is the multitude of anonymous people who have dug their hand one too many times into the drawer where the white tablets are kept. So they can sleep. So it will all stop. So they can sleep, finally sleep, confusing death with the end of suffering.

I'm not sleeping; I reach my hand toward oblivion. The world no longer exists. I am in a state of toxic, blessed numbness. I'm dying to believe that I'm falling asleep.

Another pill, and another. Repeat the same error. Sink into white forgetfulness. Into somnambulic death.

And in the effect itself of these repeated doses, the issue of sleeping pills becomes more important than that of sleep. The sleeping pill becomes salvation. "As if insomnia revealed itself to me through sleeping pills," wrote Alix Cléo Roubaud.[24] I no longer expect rest from sleep, but from the magic of the little white tablet, the insomniac's host, one's own communion.

Before she gave herself over forever to the stones and the river, Virginia Woolf was rescued, at the age of thirty-one, from an overdose of veronal, by an injection of strychnine, a lot of coffee, and whacks from a wet towel. The psychiatrist Octavia Wilberforce's prescription was a common one for women: Drink a lot of milk, eat, sleep, and do not write.[25]

Being president of the French Republic pushed Paul Deschanel into insomnia. He was forced to resign in 1920 after an overdose: under the influence of veronal, he fell from the window of a moving night train, in his pajamas, and presented himself as president to the crossing keeper, who replied that he was the Queen of England. "The absolute necessity that has been imposed on me to take a complete break," as he announced in his resignation speech, did not prevent his premature death two years later.

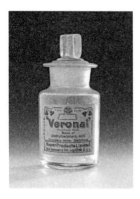

Proust twice survived overdoses of veronal and opium: "I poisoned myself (not through a death wish, loving as I do the appalling life to which I cling by a thread, but through my rage at no longer sleeping, which made me take an entire packet of veronal tablets in one go, along with Dial and opium). Rather than sleeping, I suffered terribly."[26] Suicide? How inelegant: "I would not have wanted to end up like a hero in a human interest story."[27]

Yasunari Kawabata, winner of the Nobel Prize in Literature, suffered his whole life from an addiction to sleeping pills, even falling into a coma in 1962 (ten years later he chose gas in order to fall asleep forever). In Japanese literature, accidental overdoses are so prevalent that I'd have to spend many more nights of insomnia on the topic. Kawabata even makes it the theme of his novel *The House of the Sleeping Beauties*. Clients who visit the eponymous brothel are given two sleeping tablets before they lie down to sleep beside tranquilized young girls. But what old Eguchi comes to desire above all is the same drug given to the prostitutes, the one that makes them "sleep the sleep of the dead." By the end of the novel his insomnia has worsened. "Do you expect me to sleep after this?" he exclaims as he wakes next to a girl inadvertently drugged to death. The madam proposes a replacement girl, well and truly alive, and well and truly asleep. As if death were simply a defective form of sleep. Nothing more than a simple error of dosage.

Kenzaburō Ōe, another winner of the Nobel, received the Akutagawa Prize when he was very young and, "as a consequence of this sudden entry into the life of a writer, he found himself taking strong doses of sleeping tablets."[28] In his semiautobiographical novel *A Personal Matter*, Ōe describes their effect on the main character: "Sleep for Bird was a funnel, which he entered through the wide and easy entrance and had to leave by the narrow exit … as though he had been lying in the lair of a creature whose body was constructed differently from his own."[29]

And then there are the countless suicides, those who have chosen the big sleep. When he killed himself by veronal in 1927 at the age of thirty-five, Ryūnosuke Akutagawa left a note to a friend with two key words (ten characters): "*vague* sense of *anxiety*."[30]

ぼんやりとした不安

These words are part of the collective memory in Japan. In his last short story Akutagawa describes addiction to "veronal 0.8" as being like a resting upon a sword. "He barely made it through each day in the gloom, leaning as it were upon a chipped and narrow sword."[31] The sleeping pill as the slow version of seppuku disembowelment.

Cesare Pavese committed suicide by taking twenty-two sleeping pills in Room 305 of the Hotel Roma in Turin, on the night of August 26, 1950. He was forty-two. The hotelier found him on his bed, clothed, except for his shoes. This is his last diary entry, from August 18: "Not words. An action. I shall write no more."[32]

Emmanuel Charles, *Dessin de rêve* (Dream Drawing),
April 2020

When is suicide "legitimate"? Terrible suffering? Old age? In February 2020, the French National Authority for Health recommended that midazolam, hitherto reserved for hospitals for "deep, continuous sedation until death," be henceforth available to all doctors in charge of end-of-life patients. In October 2019, 130 vials of pentobarbital, a strong sedative used on horses, had been seized during an extensive raid carried out by the French police, who had searched refrigerators in the regions of the Haute-Marne, the Médoc, and Paris, and in the homes of old people, not all of them sick, who planned to end their life when it suited them and "not be a bother to their children." They had bought their exit ticket on the internet, as it is not commercially available in France.

What a mess, what huge risks of failure, what an assault on the body if you throw yourself off a cliff, drive your car into a tree, hang yourself, drown, slit your wrists, when you could calmly, in your own bed, even surrounded by friends and family, undertake the considered action of imbibing sleep forever.

Alcohol

Sometimes alcohol helps me to live. Alcohol helps me to sleep.

Then it wakes me up. At 3:33 a.m., at 4:44 a.m., at schnapps o'clock. It's a very unpleasant time to wake up: as well as the insomnia, I have to deal with the crazy anxiety induced by alcohol poisoning, the toxic sweats, the dizziness. On these occasions, I often gulp down a Stilnox to put myself out of my misery. "It's suicide, darling," an American friend said to me. "It's suicide and it's sugar." According to this friend, panic attacks are heightened by the sugar in alcohol. I was disgusted by the idea of being stuffed full of sugar on top of the wine. That was the beginning of giving up alcohol. Back in 2016. Stopping takes time.

Because, after days of insomnia, the exhaustion is so great that at 6:00 p.m. the first glass of wine restores me to life. I immediately want another one. It's a craving, a bottomless desire, a never-ending need. Craving is preceded by obsession—the two tempos of alcohol dependence.

The first time I encountered these words was also in 2016, in the beautiful memoir *The Outrun*, by Amy Liptrot.[33] *Obsession* has the same meaning in French; *craving* is harder to translate, but the French word *crever*, "to die," reminds us that you can die from it. Amy Liptrot couldn't drink fast enough at student parties, so she went back to her place to drink alone and flat out. She was saved by a detox center (since closed) that was subsidized by the NHS, and by one of the Orkney Islands (same latitude as Oslo), where she was born and where she went to live after leaving the detox center: whenever she felt a craving, she dived into the icy sea.

One evening, during a signing session in a bookshop in Bayonne, all I could think of was the first glass of wine, the ritual toast. It was hot, I had talked a lot, the assembled readers were enthusiastic. I was empty and I wanted to fill up. The bookseller offered me a glass of txakoli, a local sparkling white that is wonderfully dry. I drank a glass along with everyone else. I immediately wanted a second, a third. Another bottle was opened for me; at my fourth glass, they were admiring my capacity for alcohol and I felt ashamed. I realized that no one—Bayonnais or not—had drunk as fast as I had.

Any excuse is good for that first drink. Whether it's loneliness or company. I'm sometimes already thinking about it at eleven in the morning. I never drink at lunchtime: I need to keep a clear mind. But I think about that first drink—the joy of it contained in a bottle—when I'm demoralized, staring at the blank page, when it's eleven o'clock in the morning, three o'clock in the afternoon, five o'clock. I sometimes go and look at my collection of pretty glasses, from my grandmother, from IKEA, from wherever, and just the sight of them gives me courage. I wait.

The obsession grows. I have a date with alcohol.

Six o'clock, *Desperate Housewives* time, when the big hand of the kitchen clock points vertically and Marcia Cross pours herself one of those enormous American glasses of wine, a bowl of red wine.

Another of my moments of realization (I needed a few of them) occurred when I read a novel by Louise Erdrich, *Shadow Tag*. The female narrator is a writer and mother of three children. Her youngest son always draws her with a strange hand, as if it had sprouted extra fingers. "It's the glass," he explains to her. The glass she always has in her hand.[34]

I began trying to drink less. In vain. My efforts simply reminded me that I was drinking every night. Not an enormous amount, of course—two or three or four glasses— but I realized I had lost the freedom not to drink. Which, alas, is the definition of alcoholism.[35]

That magic number, *two or three*—reassuring, unremarkable. Faulkner and Hemingway each knocked back their daily bottle of whisky. Marguerite Duras drank up to eight bottles of wine a day, and during the night, over the period she was writing her novella *The Malady of Death*.[36] "The worst is when you can't sleep at night.... That's when the ideal relief is alcohol. At all hours, wine. I've done it, it's excellent."[37] In 1933, Jean Rhys, an inveterate insomniac, only managed to finish her magnificent novel *Voyage in the Dark* by means of two bottles of wine a day.[38] Lawrence

Durrell talks about a Taoist master who helped him "equably, without stress" reduce his consumption of red wine to "four or five glasses a day—against a customary four or five pints."[39] And Nathalie Sarraute lived until the age of ninety-nine drinking two or three whisky-Perriers every day at afternoon tea, then smoking a dozen or so cigarettes. She treated her insomnia in the middle of the night by drinking "a small glass of vodka and a few slices of saucisson."[40]

Compared to these class acts, who am I with my *two or three* glasses? I began drinking regularly in 1996, when my first novel was published. The first whisky at seven in the evening, and the howevermanyth around midnight. In the world of books, it's mostly men who drink, but women do too, some battling to remain thin and ending up living on alcohol alone. How many times have I preferred another gimlet (150 calories: gin, sugar, lime) to dinner? *What'll it be, sir?* says Lloyd, the barman in Kubrick's film *The Shining*.

Lloyd, the barman in Kubrick's *The Shining*, 1980

I don't care that every weekend, when I get together with friends, it's five, six, seven, and eight, and then I lose count—it doesn't count. The more I drink, the less likely I am to get a hangover. I guzzle a liter of coffee; the effect of the sleeping pill mixed with that of the wine dissipates, the day begins. I curse myself, but it begins.

I stop drinking.

This evening I won't drink.

And then, off I go. I trick myself. It's not six in the evening, it's nine o'clock. The children are asleep. A little glass. And then two or three, my two or three "little" glasses of Irouléguy, of Madiran, or of Bordeaux. It's good wine, organic. That excellent Haut-Médoc, that magnificent Graves.

> Bordeaux is like a friend who in times of trouble and misfortune stands by us always, anywhere, ready to give us help, or just to share our quiet leisure. So raise your glasses—to our friend Bordeaux![41]

In 2017, a group of experts from the French Ministry of Public Health and the French National Cancer Institute recommended a maximum of ten glasses (French) of wine a week, and two days of abstinence a week—the famous liver rest and repair. The World Health Organization recommended *at least one day without alcohol.*

I can't do it.

That day without wine is interminable; it's the day I'm driven to despair. The promise of relaxation, the prospect of a glass of wine, glasses of wine, is delayed until tomorrow. Between me and that glass of wine there are still hours—hours and a whole night. A night during which I will probably not sleep.

The evening arrives. I'm totally obsessed, so irritable and agitated that I find it impossible to read or follow a conversation. I head outside for a walk, but I can't focus on anything. Sometimes going to see a film helps, sitting captive in the theatre for two hours, if the film is good. And if the actors don't drink. But my punishment intensifies as soon as I'm in bed, because I'm incapable of falling asleep without my red wine. I take a sleeping pill: Which drug is worse? In the morning, a new day begins. I'm almost serene, because this evening I'm going to drink.

As part of an anonymous survey by the French social-security system, a doctor ended my medical checkup with the standard question: "Do you have any questions?"

Why did I confess to him that I drank too much? Because arguably it's easy to say it to a stranger.

"People never really drink too much," he responded. I was astonished. "At worst," he muttered, "it puts a strain on your kidneys."

Ovid's Tears, a wine from the Tomes region,
in today's Romania, where he was exiled

"But the WHO … ," I protested.

"You can't believe everything the WHO says."

It was only when I was out in the street that I understood: he just saw me as a forty-something, middle-class leftie, mother of three, only capable of abusing mineral water and green tea.

But what I like is red wine.

My regular female GP listened to me when I finally told her that I was drinking too much. She asked how much I drank and at what times. Yes, it was too much. But I was incapable of stopping. A life of abstinence is not a life. And as to *reducing*, alas, my superego was not up for that. It was too much to ask: it was already looking after my figure, my exercise, my self-discipline, my manners; it needed to drink in order to contend with all that. My despair on the evening when I didn't drink was also too much, according to the GP. So she prescribed a medication she had already told me about: baclofen. I was a bit frightened by the name. It was a controversial drug, a muscle relaxant that also seemed to reduce cravings.[42] All I can say is that it worked for me.

I'm at a preview screening of the film *Proxima*, a beautiful film about a female astronaut, written and directed by Alice Winocour. As at all Parisian events, there is alcohol; they would be unimaginable without it. And this time, I realize in astonishment, I couldn't care less. I look at the wine in the glasses, and I even take one, to look like everyone else, and to witness the birth of this new me: I'm indifferent to the Saint-Émilion, its beautiful dark color, its bouquet. It's not disgust (as it is for a friend who, ever since his single session of hypnosis, feels nauseated at the idea of smoking). It's not that I've fallen out of love with it (I take a sip and the wine is as good as ever). It's that the wine has become an object separate from me. The wine has become part of the world, like tables, chairs, trees, the moon. It no longer has to become part of my body. I no longer have to get back into the glass, re-enter it the way a female astronaut on a mission into space, relieved to be reunited with her mothership, takes off her helmet and spacesuit, undoes her plait, shakes her hair, and can finally breathe.

How to go home without drinking? How to end my writing day without drinking? Baclofen helped me to make it through the airlock.

But a problem remains: without alcohol, I don't fall asleep. Baclofen definitely induces relaxation.[43] When my GP warned me about the drowsiness that often accompanies baclofen, I felt a surge of hope. The medication that released me from my *two or three* glasses might also, perhaps, allow me to sleep. Even the low dose of baclofen that I take, *two or three* tablets, seems to calm me. But my soothed beast is not a beast who sleeps.

I go to bed, and I don't sleep. I observe the effect of the medication with interest: minor dizziness, an enhanced hypnagogic state. But I remain vigilant, a nightlight that is never turned off.

Rituals

So instead of drinking every night, I started to increase my sleeping rituals. And to collect more reading matter on the subject. It's common knowledge that Kant was a champion obsessive, especially about his sleep: whatever was happening, he went to bed at quarter to ten and got up at five minutes to five.

Long practice had taught him a very dexterous mode of *nesting* and enswathing himself in the bedclothes. First of all, he sat down on the bedside; then with an agile motion he vaulted obliquely into his lair; next he drew one corner of the bedclothes under his left shoulder, and, passing it below his back, brought it round so as to rest under his right shoulder; fourthly, by a particular *tour d'adresse*, he operated on the other corner in the same way; and finally contrived to roll it round his whole person. Thus swathed like a mummy, or (as I used to tell him) self-involved like the silk-worm in its cocoon, he awaited the approach of sleep, which generally came on immediately.[44]

Without managing to accomplish that feat, I tuck my doona into the end of the bed in a very precise way: not too tight (that hurts my feet), not too loose (my feet get cold). Henri Michaux describes this unpleasant problem thus: "Sleep is very difficult. First of all the covers are always incredibly heavy; the bed-sheets alone are like sheet metal. If you take everything off, everyone knows what happens then. After a few minutes of sleep—undeniable for that matter—one is shot into space.... Consequently, bedtime is unparalleled torture for so many people."[45]

You can see that when I'm shot into space like that, even my astrophysicist husband has trouble sleeping with me. I am unbearable. I wear earplugs and I turn off anything that emits light. I close the shutters, I carefully pull the curtains shut; my door is covered by a wall hanging. In hotels, I wear an eye mask. I'm frightened of going to Nordic countries, with their bare windows, their individual doonas even on double beds. I leave a whole collection of herbal teas cooling on my bedside table and take two or three sips. No bladder could ever account for my innumerable comings and goings. I put lime-blossom essence on my pillow. I tie a warm scarf around my neck in winter and a sheer one in summer. Definitely no patterns on my white sheets. I have two sets of the same pajamas, so I can change them without any disruption; they bring me good luck for sleeping. Georges Perec: "Vowl is willing to try almost anything that might assist him in dozing off— a pair of pyjamas with bright polka dots, a nightshirt, a body stocking, a warm shawl, a kimono, a cotton sari from a cousin in India, or simply curling up in his birthday suit, arranging his quilt this way and that."[46]

I do a few Pilates stretches, always the same ones, with the same little inflatable ball that I also take with me when I travel. I meditate, or at least I try to. If I could, I would pray.

In *Life: A User's Manual*, Perec again, a character called Léon Marcia gets lumbered with the liturgy of insomnia: "For hours and hours the old man paces up and down in his bedroom, then goes to the kitchen to get a glass of milk from the fridge, or to the bathroom to rinse his face, or switches on the radio, at low volume but still too loud for his neighbours, to listen to crackling broadcasts from the other end of the world."[47] He's so agitated that his son has to cover the party wall with strips of cork.

Here is Philip Roth in *Asymmetry*, the novel by Lisa Halliday: "He would switch off the phone, the fax, the lights, pour himself a glass of chocolate soymilk, and count out a small pile of pills. 'The older you get,' he explained, 'the more you have to do before you can go to bed. I'm up to a hundred things.'"[48] The glass of chocolate soy milk stayed with me. I tried out several brands. The vanilla-tasting one is thick and sugary, very palatable; it weighs a little on the stomach but digestion is conducive to sleep. It's no substitute for the Saint-Émilion, but it keeps my mind off things and it's a lot cheaper. I can use pretty cups, or even glasses, although I don't go as far as stemmed glasses. And soy milk is apparently excellent for women of my age. In short, Philip Roth has found a female fan.

Des Esseintes, Huysmans's famous character, also employs innumerable extreme measures: "He had without success tried to install equipment for hydrotherapy in his dressing-room.... Since he could not be scourged by jets of water which, smacking and drumming directly at his dorsal vertebrae, were the only thing powerful enough to quell his insomnia and restore his tranquillity, he was reduced to brief aspersions in his bath-tub or sitz bath, to simple cold affusions followed by vigorous rub-downs by his manservant with a horsehair glove.... To amuse himself and fill the interminable hours, he turned to his boxes of prints and sorted his Goyas."[49]

Not everyone has Goyas to arrange. But between downing a glass of hot milk and immersing oneself in an icy bath, the rituals of insomniacs are often sadomasochistic: Quake in your boots, you wretch—now you're going to sleep! André Gide, in his journal: "Insomnia, I am struggling as best I can; force myself to 'take exercise'; to walk, to take a cold tub as soon as I return from a 'health walk.' ... Nothing does any good; each night is a bit worse than the preceding one."[50] The protagonist in Mari Akasaka's novel *Vibrator*, which I like a lot, makes herself vomit in order to sleep.[51] I had never heard of that. Something to do with endorphins. And in Chuck Palahniuk's *Fight Club*, the narrator, haggard with insomnia, attends meetings of patients suffering from shocking illnesses he doesn't have, invasive cancers, parasitic brain infections ... and discovers that listening to them puts him to sleep.

Henri Michaux: "All night long, I push a wheelbarrow ... it's so cumbersome. And on this wheelbarrow sits a huge toad ... it's so heavy, and its body gets bigger as the night goes on."[52]

Lists

Instead of pushing the toad of insomnia or going through a series of complicated rituals, one can always make lists. "Counting sheep" is the metaphor for this routine. One word, one thing. One sheep, one second of time. A benign animal, a herd of certainties.

A list promises security. Reality adheres to language. Time passes via the needle eye of words.

In "Now I Lay Me," a story in Hemingway's collection *Men without Women*, the narrator relives one by one every trout-fishing trip he's been on. He makes lists in his head of all the animals he knows, all the birds, fish, countries, cities, and all the different kinds of food he's eaten, the names of all the streets in Chicago, and finally all the girls he could have or should have married (his companion promises him that marriage cures insomnia). Finally, he goes back to trout fishing and streams because he's less likely to get muddled with them. "Some nights too I made up streams."[53]

The protagonist in Kawabata's novella *The House of the Sleeping Beauties* also brings to the surface of his insomniac memory, one by one, every girl he has ever slept with. I too try to remember names, I ask myself Bill Clinton–type questions (what actually constitutes "sexual relations" again?), I list my lovers and usually get to about thirty. Is

Juliana Dorso, *Portrait de R. endormie* (Portrait of R. sleeping), April 2020

that a large or a small number for a European woman born in 1969? I note in any case that the number has tended to diminish over time.

A list reduces names to objects. Pearls. Stitches in knitting. Notches on the rifle butt. Meaning is erased, lived time is compressed. You can't think when you're counting. You can't turn things over in your mind when you're chanting. The mind's compactor gets jammed by the cadence.

Then I count my babysitters, of whom, oddly enough, I have had the same number as lovers, and the memory of them is sometimes as emotional, the connections are as strong (lifelong) or as fleeting (a single night), their first names I remember particularly well (because, unlike my lovers, my babysitters were at some point recorded in my mobile phone, an object that wasn't always around when I had lovers, but was always there when I had babies). Anyway …

Count Robert de Montesquiou-Fezensac (engraving by Henri Guérard, after Whistler)

I think I'm going to fall asleep,
but I don't fall asleep.

The very elegant Robert de Montesquiou, who was the
inspiration for both Huysmans's Des Esseintes and
Proust's Charlus, was a dandy who exhibited innumerable
idiosyncratic mannerisms, and an immensely wealthy art
collector. Beauty had to reign in his home at all times,
even during "a minute of insomnia": he slept or attempted
to sleep by the light of a porcelain cat transformed into a
night light, "the back of which was perforated in a symmetrical rose shape, through which luminous pictures
were projected, enlarged, onto the ceiling."[54] This aesthete
wrote ten volumes of poetry, including these two lines on
sleep: "An apprenticeship for our future death / And every
night man confronts his grave."

Obsession, like lists, means death, the blood's circulation
reduced to a trickle, our bed transformed into a coffin.
Obsessional insomniacs organize their nights like burials.
A never-ending *To be, or not to be*. Hamlet's famous mono-
logue oscillates between life and death, between sleeping
and dying: "To die, to sleep— / No more; and by a sleep
to say we end / The heart-ache."[55]

Yes, yes, to sleep is to die a little: this truism is one of the
keys to insomnia. If tonight is to be the last night, it would
be better to stay awake … Already in Homer, sleep and

death—Hypnos and Thanatos, the "swift messengers"—are twins.[56] "My room seemed like a tomb," said Xavier de Maistre, better known for having written in a lighter mood.[57] In *The Blind Owl*, Sadegh Hedayat's narrator describes his feelings of suffocation: "Several times the thought that I was in a coffin had occurred to me. At night my room seemed to shrink and press in on me from all sides. Isn't this the same as the feeling that one experiences in the grave?"[58] And Borges in his poem "Insomnia": "These six narrow walls filled with narrow eternity are stifling me." Indeed, the box has six sides: four walls, a floor, and a ceiling.

It's all very well knowing it; we scarcely sleep any better.

And there's always that friend who opens the doors to his old stone house and tells you that "everyone sleeps well when they come here." In the morning he holds it against you personally that you're the only one on whom his granite walls haven't had a positive effect. And there's always that friend, especially one who sleeps well, who gives you advice, lists of things to do. Podcasts from the Collège de France. Whale songs. The radio, but in foreign languages. Masturbation. Sleeping with your feet elevated.

I only listen to serious insomniacs, because they dance with death. "I've tried everything," the artist Gilles Barbier writes to me, "pills, whisky, sport, belly breathing, 'goodnight' herbal teas, passionflower tea … It's no use … Of course, behind this empty time a little game with death is playing out. By sleeping four hours a night I calculated that, every six days, I was gaining twenty-four waking hours, twenty-four hours of conscious living. That is, 1.666 days a week and 86.632 days a year. So, over the forty-one years I've been an insomniac, that comes to 3,551.972 days, or 6.731 years that I've gained. Which gives me a decent head start. Nevertheless, I sometimes wonder if some kind of biological justice won't settle the score in the end. To be continued …"

Gilles Barbier, *Squeezed Head*, 2010

I've Tried Everything

I too have tried everything in order to sleep.

I've tried herbal teas. Whole fields of them. Not a single one puts me to sleep. Just the idea of them amuses me. But there are some very good ones.

I've tried acupuncture. An old Chinese doctor stuck needles in my skeptical ankle and told me to lie down. The table was hard. I was cold. I fell asleep immediately. When he woke me twenty minutes later, I was astonished. Unfortunately, this extraordinary result had absolutely no impact on my ability to sleep at night. He would have to have come every evening and jabbed needles in my ankle.

I've tried cranial osteopathy. The following night, I sleep like a log. The night after, my illness takes hold of me again. I would need to have these treatments every evening in my bed, like a princess.

I've tried psychoanalysis, which saved my life but did nothing to put me to sleep.

I've tried yoga nidra, on the advice of Elin Tobiassen, my Norwegian translator: "You are perhaps a 'yang' person; your mind is 'boiling,' even at night … Personally, I now manage to relax completely in the evening, I let the world go on without me, I don't think about anything anymore. Yoga nidra helped me a lot." My body unwinds, borne by the voice of the teacher, upside-down-chair pose (or frog, or downward dog, or dead body ...), gong-and-birdsong soft music. This yoga does indeed allow one to reach a deep state of relaxation. One of the most important gods in the Indian pantheon is sleeping Vishnu. The very spirit of the world, he floats over the primordial waters ... It's not exactly sleep but a way of being in the present ... At the end of half an hour of our graceful collective efforts, I start to envision places. The others probably see things that relate to them, perhaps places too? In any case, my places are empty, a bit like De Chirico's paintings, and often from the Basque region and insignificant. The entrance to a freeway. The small carpark in front of the greengrocer's. The bridge before the vineyards. I'm not driving around—that's not what I mean. It's more as if I'm letting the places where I drive pass through me. Perhaps the turn-off toward sleep is passing through me. But I don't sleep.

I've tried meditation. Inhaling-exhaling, blood pounding ... a rhythm without a subject, to rescue the insomniac in the grip of rehashing things ... Yes, becoming that intense point of focus that breathes as time sees fit ... "Let go": allow the ebb and flow of the lungs, the pendulum of the heart to take their course ... Pleasant enough during the daytime, meditation has become a 24/7 big business, as we rush to meditation retreats marked in our diaries. At 4:04

a.m., during the ghastly rendezvous with myself, meditation infuriates me.

I've tried fasting. Both food and digital. I stayed in an old monastery; it was so quiet that at night I heard my heart beating. I slept very badly the first five nights, as I withdrew from everything, including sleeping pills. The sixth night I slept the whole night through and woke up stunned, bright-eyed and bushy-tailed (that hadn't happened for a very long time) and late for morning yoga. This is what I had to do in order to sleep: deprive myself of all stimulants, including food; walk fifteen kilometers a day (they used the Buchinger method of fasting and walking); one after the other have a massage, a sauna, vegetable broth, then go to bed. It took me all day long to be able to sleep at night. I had scarcely returned to normal life than the demon 4:00 a.m. returned. According to the shiatsu masseur in this very special monastery, "Four in the morning is the hour of the liver."

I've tried hypnosis.[59] My two attempts in this area—one with an Ericksonian hypnotherapist, the other with a Californian artist—induced powerful states of relaxation, but I didn't sleep. My stubborn little consciousness persisted in examining not my own case but the situation itself—the "character" of the hypnotherapist, the décor around us, the novel he might or might not give rise to. There was a therapeutic benefit in terms of my boredom, but scarcely at all in regard to my insomnia.

Artist Marcos Lutyens's hypnosis cabin at dOCUMENTA, Kassel, 2012. The floor isn't made of mirrors but is the symmetrical bottom section of the cabin. Sessions took place on the steps.

I've tried the sensation without a name. In *A Brief Stay with the Living*, I attempted to evoke it:

> yes, a soft sensation, a wave rising up along the skull,
> shrinking the scalp ... a process of head-shrinking ...
> tingling skin ... anything will do ... a soft, regular
> motion, something unbroken, which goes on, swinging,
> sleepy, to and fro, rocking ... rising along the skull,
> between skin and bone ... it's rising, like a laying on of
> hands, and her thoughts become detached, start floating,
> she likes that, her fingers and lips grow heavy ... her
> languid eyelids fall, her neck relaxes, shoulders recede
> below her heavy yet airy head ...[60]

The numerous people who feel and who try to describe this unique sensation form a nameless community, now associated with the initialism ASMR (an awful abbreviation), Autonomous Sensory Meridian Response, also known as the "tingle community." In optimal conditions, the sensation travels down the neck and shoulders and can reach the belly, the thighs, and induce a form of intense pleasure that I personally have always distinguished from sexual pleasure (not all accounts agree on this point). Lots of research groups attempt to understand it, and countless YouTube videos try to elicit it. The ArkDes museum in Stockholm devoted an exhibition to it in 2020: *Weird Sensation Feels Good.* There is a lot of debate between those who think it is conducive to sleep, and those who don't (I'm in the latter group).

I've tried the gravity blanket. Despite its grand name, suggestive of space and gravity, this is an extremely heavy blanket, a sort of large comforter invented by a young American entrepreneur. I was hoping to recreate the miracle of *one of the most wonderful nights of my life* (insomniacs marvel at a good night's sleep more than they do a night of love). That most wonderful night was spent jetlagged and in a state of malaise in a ryokan, an inn in Kyoto, where I had just arrived. It was freezing on my hard tatami mat, the walls were made of paper, the quilt was too thin, and it was a double room. I had the idea of covering myself with the second tatami, so I was sandwiched between two mattresses. A tatami mat is very heavy. I was sound asleep in no time.

The company I contacted for my gravity blanket was financed by an online community group, and the blankets were made to order according to the size and weight of the customer. First up, I received a lot of emails from the young entrepreneur (in China) about the manufacturing problems; finally, the very heavy blankets set off on their flight across the planet. Mine arrived at Roissy Airport but was held up because of customs charges. I paid the fees and went, on the tram, to collect it from a warehouse at the Porte de Vanves, less than half an hour from my place, forgetting that, according to the manufacturer's instructions, its weight constituted fifteen percent of my own. The whole process had already caused me a fair amount of fatigue, but fatigue, alas, has never put insomniacs to sleep. All the same, for €250, I was able to let myself be crushed by a blanket as long and as wide as me (my arms stuck by my sides). I wondered if the sensation of being squashed would bring back uterine memories. In any case, it was difficult to be restless. On the first night, my knee got stuck in a painful position: I woke up. On the second night, I hadn't secured the blanket well enough and it fell on the ground, *bang*. I woke up. On the third night, the weight was so badly distributed (the blanket is usually filled with micro glass beads) that it smothered me at chest level but left my feet sticking up in the air. The anti-insomnia blanket prevented me from sleeping.

The Morphée box

I tried the Morphée Relaxation and Sleep Aid Device. "The non-digital invention that will help you to go to sleep and to sleep better." It has my name on it. For seventy-nine euros, the object, sent from Aix-en-Provence, is beautiful, round, made of metal and beech wood, and the gentle sounds it emits are just about to transport me to the sensation without a name. I am completely relaxed, in darkness, without phone or screen; the wood is speaking to me. But already sentences are forming in my head (despite the voice telling me to concentrate, in that moment, on my left toe), the feeling of living an experience *for the book I'm writing* prevents me from sleeping, I'm already mentally writing this paragraph, I am about to get up and take notes, especially as the pretty box contains no fewer than 210 different exercises, just like a box of chocolates. I try all the *cardiac coherence* exercises; the muscular fibers of my heart relax, and when I finish turning the big keys on the box I feel marvelous and it is four o'clock in the morning.

I've tried the Champ de Fleurs acupressure mat, covered in stimulators in the form of peaked petals. "The intense pressure felt from lying on the mattress produces relief through the emission of endorphins, which act as pain relief and as a relaxant as strong as morphine but produced by your own brain … Deep relaxation, improved sleep … do not miss out on the Champ de Fleurs experience." That also has my name on it. I buy the cushion as well, discounted if you get both (€159 for the package). Following the instructions, I roll out the mat on the floor and lie down half-naked. It's extremely painful. Then I feel intense heat spreading along my back. I start to float, my old injuries easing so much that I feel as if I'm shrinking. Yes, I am relaxed. It lasts an hour. My indifferent family walks around me. With my hair shirt on, I go so far as to slide the mattress into my bed, like the nuns who engaged in mortification of the flesh. But I don't fall asleep.

The nibs of the Champ de Fleurs, made
in Latvia by the company Bioloka

I would have liked to try the Dreem headband, invented by Hugo Mercier, a young entrepreneur "out to conquer sleep," but it was out of stock. The sleepless—we are not alone.

I tried the Alexander Technique, a gentle postural realignment that teaches you how to, literally, better carry your head on your body. The British diplomat Sir Stafford Cripps was one of the first beneficiaries of the technique at the beginning of the nineteenth century. "Instead of feeling one's body to be an aggregation of ill-fitting parts, full of friction and dead weights pulling this way and that, so as to render mere existence in itself exhausting, the body becomes a coordinated and living whole, composed of well-fitting and truly articulated parts." The technique is useful for those with stiff shoulders and particularly appeals to musicians. It helps me to write better. But I don't sleep better.

I've tried metaphors. "Think like a mountain," said Aldo Leopold: if the wolves don't eat a few deer, the deer will eat all the trees and the soil from the mountains will flow into the rivers.[61] Thinking like a mountain is to accept not being *completely* safe. Welcoming *a little bit* of danger. I tell myself that a good sleep would be *to sleep like a mountain.* Stable, but with a few wolves roaming across my quivering skin. Accept the wolves, even in my dreams, so they don't wake me up … Oh, metaphors, metaphors … I visualize a mountain, deer, wolves; soon there'll be sheep. Renaude Gosset, my Alexander Technique therapist, told me that in order to get back to sleep at night she tried to *stay on the surface of her skin* … That phrase helps me. I try, yes I try, in my four-o'clock-in-the-morning insomnia, to stay on the surface of my skin. It's a high-wire act. And, every now and again, the phrase stops me from diving back inside my head.

I've tried reading. But reading makes me dive into other heads and keeps me awake. In *A Journey round My Skull*, Frigyes Karinthy laments that there does not exist a means, in order to fall asleep without drugs, to discover "the precise point in my imaginative apparatus—somewhere down in the region of the pituitary body—where the whole brain centre could be automatically anaesthetized and, as it were, prised up out of reality, with its workings stilled, much as Archimedes proposed to lever the globe."[62] Just like my first husband, an insomniac mathematician, who, during his long periods of wakefulness, would fantasize about a system of a hammer on pulleys above the bed. The hammer would strike exactly in the middle of his forehead, right at the spot he hoped was the center of his unattainable sleep.

I've tried to slow down. But I like to go fast.

And *I've tried marriage* (twice), but the career of my second husband, who is even faster than I am, at various times involves speeding up particles.

I would like to try the sleep accelerator. The machine that gets you to sleep fast. Bombarded with ions, pulverized at an unheard-of speed, I would rematerialize at the end of the enormous loop, completely recast, reborn—asleep.

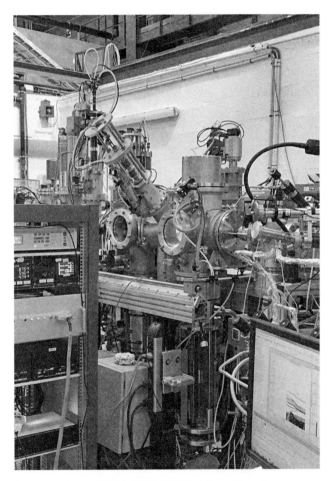

Particle accelerator, IGLIAS, GANIL-CIMAP platform, Caen, France

III

Zones, Abysses, Ravines

But I am wakeful, my endless woes are wakeful too.
                                                    —Ovid[1]

The insomniac lies there waiting for the gray of dawn,
which to him signifies the damnation not only of him alone
in his insomniac hell but of all misbegotten humanity rele-
gated to the wrong planet ...
                                                    —*Peter Handke*[2]

"There's only one dream a night," said the painter Sam Francis. I don't know exactly what that sentence means. But it has the poetic power of dreams. On a single rotation in the world's whirling night, are all the dreams of human beings in the end the same dream? Or seven and a half billion dreams and nightmares?

The Dream Zone

Dreams come to good sleepers in the time it takes to say "I'm falling asleep." Once their head hits the pillow they scarcely have a moment to explore the half-asleep, half-awake state that is the hypnagogic zone. The young officer in *The Tartar Steppe* is supposed to keep watch … and then … and then … "he saw a great hall, a horse on a white road; he seemed to hear voices calling him by name and fell asleep."[3]

For good sleepers, this zone is a fairly happy place. In *A Journey around My Room*, Xavier de Maistre insists that his valet follow a morning ritual of waking him but letting him go back to sleep for a good half an hour: "I hear him moving about my room with a light step, and stealthily managing his preparations. This noise just suffices to convey to me the pleasant knowledge that I am slumbering—a delicate pleasure this, unknown to most men. You are just awake enough to know you are not entirely so, and to make a dreamy calculation that the hour for business and worry is still in the sand-glass of time."[4] It's hard to believe that this dissolute chap is in prison in Turin.

But the zone is not all happiness. Those who sleep badly spend much more than *half an hour* there. They experience the tiresome "continuity of parks."[5] They have to contend with escarpments. They hurtle down slopes. Kafka in his *Diaries*: "I cannot sleep. Only dreams, no sleep. Today, in my dream, I invented a new kind of vehicle for a park slope."[6]

Insomnia is a ravine where those looking for sleep do battle with shadows and charge down screes. The insomniac is like the prince slashing his sword through a forest of thorns, tirelessly seeking the way to Sleeping Beauty's castle.

In *Night Roads*, Clément Rosset attests to this painful downward slide: "These hypnagogic daydreams, which should, as the word's etymology indicates (*upnos*, sleep; *agô*, lead to) lead me to sleep, 'derail' me, one after the other and, instead of resolving in sleep, they immediately make way for a new hypnagogic theme that will be no more successful than the last one."[7] *Night Roads* is nothing more than the collection of these exhausting dreams, which could end up exhausting the reader, who, in the depths of her sleepless night, remembers Henry James's famous reproof: "tell a dream, lose a reader."

And Kafka, definitely the master of the zone, on October 2, 1911: "Sleepless night. The third in a row. I fall asleep soundly, but after an hour I wake up, as though I had laid my head in the wrong hole. I am completely awake, have the feeling that I have not slept at all or only under a thin skin, have before me anew the labor of falling asleep and feel myself rejected by sleep.... I sleep along-side myself, so to speak, while I myself must struggle with dreams. About five, the last trace of sleep is exhausted, I just dream, which is more exhausting than wakefulness. In short, I spend the whole night in that state in which a healthy person finds himself for a short time before really falling asleep."[8]

Caretaker of his own desert, the insomniac does his rounds by keeping watch over himself. Neither asleep nor awake, he goes round and round in the dark, a sentinel watching over sleep that never comes ... on the lookout for ghosts ... he is a lotus-eater ... "an aqueduct-blaster."[9] Insomnia is a folie à deux: a severed head looks at me on the pillow, and that head is me.

Oh, my insomnia, what plan are you following? Do we need to marshal this huge turmoil of ghosts? I'm writing this at four o'clock in the morning. Leap over the ravines of these pages, sleep if you can, come and find me again after I loop the loop.

Loopings

Sleeping means trusting the night, believing in a reunion after the commotion of dreams. But, as Anne Dufour-mantelle told me, "you become neurotic when you confuse today with tomorrow." Insomnia is believing that *because I am not sleeping, I will never sleep.* Insomnia feeds itself on the fear of not sleeping; the conviction of exhausted exhaustion. The nightmare of the day ahead casts a shadow over the night that will end only in the nightmare of the day ahead … All this looping the loop, yes, all this figure-eight rollercoasting pitches you downhill to the point of vertigo, of senselessness.

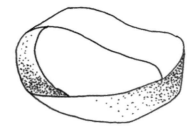

Ruban de Möbius (Möbius strip), drawing by Yann Denier

Sleepless nights take on the shape of a Möbius strip. The single-sided, single-edged surface continues unen-dingly, looping back on itself. "I dream that I dream that my sleeplessness has been destroyed," sings Barbara (1975), and one of her young successors, Pomme (2017):

> And the less I sleep, the more I think
> And the more I think the less I forget
> The vast dead end, the vast space
> That awaits me at the bottom of my bed.[10]

I think that I think that I think that I think. *Here, here, here,* a screw rams into my forehead … *right now, now, now,* a saw slices me into bits of the present. "We are held to being, held to be," wrote Levinas. "Vigilance is absolutely empty of all object. Vigilance is as anonymous as the night itself."[11] No opening where I can escape from myself: I am I, and I would so like to be someone else, someone who sleeps … Relieve me of my consciousness, the appalling consciousness of sleeplessness.

Insomnia is one of the spiraled forms of anxiety. In the bottomless room, the walls pulsate. They move away and they come closer. They shed their molecules in a shower. A black cloud fills the black air. I breathe in the atoms of the walls. I become those atoms. As the night is pulverized, it grinds me up. I am kneaded into the material from which black holes are made, I dissolve in the antimatter of the underside of the world.

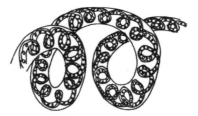

Sketch from *My Phantom Husband*, Marie Darrieussecq

Peter Handke: "Even now I sometimes wake up with a start, as though in response to some inward prodding, and, breathless with horror, feel that I am literally rotting from second to second. The air in the darkness is so still that, losing their balance, torn from their moorings, the things of my world fly soundlessly about: in another

Emmelene Landon-Otchakovsky, *Naufrage* (Shipwreck), 2010

minute they will come crashing down from all directions and smother me."[12]

In *The N-Word of the Narcissus*, the short novel by Joseph Conrad, horizontal and vertical coordinates are turned upside down.[13] A storm. The land is far away. James Wait, whose surname is significant, will spend the whole voyage apart from the others. Is he sick? Is he escaping a racist crew? He is accused, like Jonas, of having summoned headwinds. Shipwreck. His bunkbed becomes a trap. The ship has capsized. With the deck in the air, the masts down, the men scramble about on rigging that until now had been vertical. A mental plumb line and good sea legs are needed to read this seesawing. Wait, struggling under a jumble of toppling objects, bangs into the walls of his cabin. *There was no sleep on board that night.*

Insomnia. The water is no longer the horizon. The deck is no longer the ground. Interminable backwashing. Morning will never come again. Walking on doors. Standing on the ceiling. Your foot on someone else's chest. Time flies off the handle and disaster flows in through shocking holes in the hull. The insomniac is not so much in dialogue with sleep as with the apocalypse.

Capsules and Black Holes

Where did I see that cartoon, perhaps fittingly by Mœbius (pseudonym of the contemporary French artist Jean Giraud), in which the characters wander around lost, not in the nighttime, but in the vast emptiness of the white page? Latitude and longitude: a void. Horizontal and vertical coordinates: *nihil.* No more up, no more down. Avalanche survivors talk about a total disorientation: Which way to start digging; where is the way out? This apparent given in our existence—the sense of where the ground is, where the sky is—is not self-evident. Gravity can abandon us, and so can sidedness, our left and our right. As a child, playing in a darkened room, it's terrifying no longer knowing which way up the bed is. You have to turn the light on to work out where you are. The only solution is to have a rest, so that the bed, the other pieces of furniture, the window, your body, can fall into place again. Just as the sand beneath our feet, or the glimpse of sky through the snow, restores the world to us.

And yet, for insomniacs, turning on the light serves no purpose. Insomnia is still there, inside and outside. The grid pattern of our mental geography remains full of holes. Neither time nor space is "settled." That shadow near the door remains suspicious. The bedroom is warped. Space is dilated like our pupils. The house seems different, the same but different. The wearying familiarity of disturbing strangeness.

"Darkness moved slowly through my body. I tossed and turned in the bed, trying to escape from something that was already part of me."[14] Almost all the characters in the novels of the Norwegian writer Nikolaj Frobenius are insomniacs. He also wrote the screenplay of the film *Insomnia*, in which Al Pacino plays a cop who can't sleep.[15] In Nightmute, a real village of two hundred inhabitants in Alaska, it is always summer. Pacino sticks blankets, paper bags, cardboard boxes up against the window, but he can't sleep. It's the sun. In his case, it's also an unsolved murder that haunts him. Insomnia unfolds its own night within us.

So, how to get total blackness? Roller shutter, double glazing … And then earplugs. Not much of an arsenal. Some nights, a sensory-deprivation chamber seems like the ideal solution.

I am in the space capsule, the ubiquitous capsule from science-fiction films and novels.

Take *High Life*, the 2018 film by Claire Denis, in which a group of criminals on death row are sent on a mission through space to seek a renewable energy source. Juliette Binoche plays a deranged doctor who administers an injection to the crew: everyone falls asleep. Except the pilot, a fine boned, petite blonde on the edge of her bunkbed, one hand cupped under her delicate head. She resists all potions.

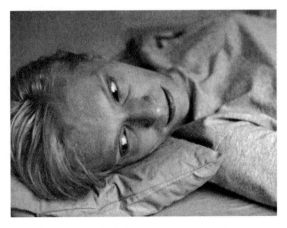

Agata Buzek as the pilot in *High Life*, dir. Claire Denis

"I'm the pilot. You can't make me sleep."

I am the pilot, but the pilot of nothing. I'm tacking back and forth in an aquarium. I am the fish-pilot of my bedroom, the suckerfish sticking to the walls, suctioned onto the roof. I am the pilot of oblivion. No one will make me sleep.

At the beginning of the film *Alien*, the seven crew members of the space tug *Nostromo* emerge, as the lids of their individual pods open. Their cryogenic sleep has been interrupted. It is far too early in their interstellar night, a long way from their port of destination. It's the equivalent of four in the morning … That's a bad sign. At the end of the massacre, the only survivor, Ripley, returns to her pod, to stasis, for a very deep sleep. Until she awakes for the next film.

Stasis—it's what I dream of, all functions suspended except the vital ones. Sleep at the speed of light. Cruising in a limitless space. Floating in the ocean of the universe. If my bedroom is a space shuttle, if my bed is a bunk in a spacecraft, the central computer has abandoned ship. I am waltzing around by myself. *My mind is going, Dave. I can feel it.*

2001: A Space Odyssey. Toing and froing among the planets. In order to save the mission, HAL the computer has to disconnect the humans. So Dave the human has to disconnect HAL. It's the clash of two forms of intelligence, two visions of the mission. *You will sleep! I will not sleep!* The skull is a space vessel. I follow competing orders from the spaceship. I do battle with myself. I want to disconnect myself. It's either me or me. Something has to give.

Sleep!

Flip a switch! Or remove the hard disks of my memory, one by one, the way Dave wipes out HAL, and slide into the void.

At times, in the madness of no sleep, it's like oscillating between two worlds. Alive but in a dead-end life, without birth, without death, a moment that is both static and spinning. The cosmonaut in *2001* becomes a fetus again in order to die. Those quantum-physics experiments in which, in the same moment, the same electron passes through two holes at a time, have a truth about them, at night, that gravity no longer has. The world is on the cusp. Time is on hold. We speak to ghosts and spirits. When it was released, Kubrick's film bewildered critics; for insomniacs it was the film of their life.

Visitors

"Impossible to sleep" is the third sentence in *The Invention of Morel*, the slim, brilliant novel by Adolfo Bioy Casares.[16] A fugitive is shipwrecked on a deserted island. The deserted island is not deserted; it is populated, but only on and off. The fugitive understands that the tides trigger a machine beneath the island that projects holograms of people long dead. There is no sleep when the emptiness is inhabited.

The monster comes when we're asleep. He takes advantage of our sleeping to make his appearance. In the bedroom. In the ship. In our dreams. It's enough to make us keep our eyes open. Insomniacs are familiar with this cliché in horror films: the only way to escape Freddy in *A Nightmare on Elm Street* is to stay awake. Going to bed for an insomniac is like being the narrator in Edgar Allan Poe's short story "The Premature Burial": "Alas! the grim legion of sepulchral terrors cannot be regarded as altogether fanciful; but, like the Demons in whose company Afrasiab made his voyage down the Oxus, they must sleep or they will devour us; they must be suffered to slumber, or we perish."[17]

Hidden in our attics, lurking under our mattresses, sitting on our chests, heavy and hideous, standing guard over us, is the demon who never sleeps.

All our body wants is to sleep. It wants to leave us, head back to the stable, a worn-out horse. Who are these visitors that take us away from ourselves?

> I'm frightened of shadows
> I'm frightened of everything
> The man in black. The black mask.
> The black cape, the black gloves.
> Is he coming?[18]

Niki de Saint Phalle calligraphed her poem "Insomnie" (Insomnia).

The aging Immanuel Kant was an insomniac, besieged by ghosts. "There must be no yielding to panics of darkness," he urged himself in his notebook.[19] "Don't switch [the light] off, Céleste. There's a big fat woman in the room … a horrible big fat woman in black."[20] At the end of his life, Proust did battle with this shadow. A dead woman also visited Sadegh Hedayat every night. Whether it be a succubus or a ghost, in all languages, these are our night passengers, our insomniac torments, our uninvited guests.

I can't remember who wrote that great short story about an enormous clawed beast with fangs, probably hanging from the ceiling, that drops on top of a hotel guest, who fights and kills it, the duel leaving him covered in wounds. He turns on the light: nothing. The hotel room is empty. He trips over an unseen corpse. À la Pompeii, he coats it in plaster, almost lovingly. It dries, a solid shroud. When he removes the mold and pours wax into the cavity, the shape appears: it's the beast in relief, the unnamable in plain view. Was it Lovecraft? Poe? Or another writer who flushed out monsters?

Inside the space station in Andrei Tarkovsky's *Solaris*, 1972

On the planet Solaris, in a distant future, no one sleeps. Stanislaw Lem, the Polish author of the eponymous novel, imagines a vast ocean of sentient gel, which delivers to its explorers the thing they miss the most. What Kelvin misses most is his wife. He is a widower. She comes back. There she is. It's her. Her body. Her voice. Her speech. Her breath. They make love. Her skin is warm. Her heart beats. Her blood is red, but under the microscope not one of her atoms has a nucleus. She is nothing but an empty simulacrum, a pure phantom. His wife who is not his wife and who is still his wife is a being made of plasma, formed from the ocean itself.

And yet "she has already learnt to sleep." It's one of the most terrifying sentences I know.[21] This spume humanoid already knows how to imitate us at our most intimate. The ocean surges on, imperturbable. Everyone stays isolated in their cabins with their own phantom, fascinated, seduced, terrified. And all the while she already knows how to surrender to the strange sea that is sleep. Something insomniacs can't do.

Ghosts

On December 20, 1921, Kafka was "startled out of a deep sleep. By the light of a candle, I saw a strange man sitting at a little table in the centre of the room. Broad and heavy, he sat in the dim light, his unbuttoned winter coat making him appear even broader."[22] Already on October 2, he had been visited by a little girl, or a little boy, he couldn't tell which, only that the child was very young, and half-blind. And elsewhere he wrote this: "A small ghost, a child, appeared at the end of the dark corridor. That visit was all that was missing, because if truth be told I was waiting."

For years, I've kept that quote, written in one of my note-books, for a book waiting to be written, a book that will perhaps be called *A Ghost*, or *Only the Ghosts*, or *My Parents' Son*, or *The Sister without a Brother*. Or another title that will emerge? For a thousand reasons, this book is not being written. Will I manage to sleep the day I have written it?

Would I sleep if I were not haunted by this child? And if others around me weren't? And what does *haunted* mean?

I read and reread Kafka's *Diaries*, in the two editions I own, but I can't find that quote. Does it come from his correspondence? It's a ghost quote. One day it will come to me. It will be like a visit that, if truth be told, I've been expecting. We open books and they speak to us, especially at night. We can always count on pages opening by themselves; there's no such thing as chance in libraries; books sitting side by side talk to each other. Echoes. And we don't sleep.

"Ah! If it's that baby you mean, he's been installed on an efficient conveyer system in an infant slaughterhouse and is weakening to death this very minute—well, that's proba-bly for the best!"[23] Written faraway, and two years earlier than the death of their child, it is the story of my parents and their son.

I never shared a room with my parents' son. I grew up without him in my childhood home. A haunted house, obviously. And since the birth of my own children, insomnia has traveled everywhere with me. It has attached itself to me like a small ghost. It follows me wherever I go. And it has become sly. It has contaminated others around me.

My maternal grandmother, Amaxi, saw ghosts. She too had lost her firstborn. But it was her daughter-in-law, my aunt, who visited her at dawn. My aunt, with her blonde perm, sat on the edge of my grandmother's bed in her blue skirt and jacket with gold buttons. She had suicided a few months earlier. My grandmother only talked about these visits with my mother, who in turn talked to me about them. Amaxi was not mad and was not lying. She was "in the zone." We could choose to follow her, or not. I believed her and I didn't believe her. But the words of my dead aunt, as reported by Amaxi, were always spot on.

> "In other words," says Rose, "families who refuse the benefits of psychology are more inclined to produce individuals who are open to witnessing supernatural phenomena?"
>
> "That's it," says Arnaud. "Sometimes, in order to speak of the dead, the only solution is to see them."[24]

I do what I can with all that. I stir it all in my cauldron. I've also been a psychoanalyst.

I'm walking with my mother and father, one on either side of me. We arrive at the Zugarramurdi pass, where I place one foot in Spain and one foot in France. I stand there, waiting to feel something. I'm five years old. The rolling countryside around me is green and wet. The landscape is the same on both sides. Native Basque ponies, *pottoks*, are grazing; the oak forest couldn't care less about the border. Beneath my feet, the Cave of the Witches (who are called *sorginak* in Basque), where they held their sabbath (*akelarre* in Basque), joins up with the Caves of Sare. The Basque chasms form a single labyrinth.

Amaxi had a job as a *ramendeuse*: she repaired the fishing nets when the trawlers came in, from four in the morning onward, at the port of Saint-Jean-de-Luz. I was fascinated by her amazing ability to sleep. She would close the shutters very early and go to sleep lying on her right ear because she was deaf in her left (the result of a bad ear infection when she was forty). In her private silence, she slept for as long as she needed. I don't think the ghosts woke her up. They waited until she was awake to visit her.

Her aunt, my great-great-aunt, who wore a mantilla and high heels, was a fortune teller and conducted séances. History doesn't record whether she slept or not. She must

Amaxi was always elegant.

have been gifted with some powerful energy because, during one wild session, a coffee table went sailing through the window.

My paternal grandmother had been a milliner before devoting herself to home duties. Devoting herself for better or for worse, because she was in all likelihood psychotic. At the time, no one delivered diagnoses such as that when it came to a housewife who was certainly strange but whose household held together, more or less. *She was mad as a hatter.* And she was an insomniac. She used to press an acupuncture point just below her wrist. She had seen on TV that this procedure helped people to sleep. I remember her sitting with her hands joined in an odd position, murmuring, as if praying for sleep.

She talked in circles, or spirals. She would start at one point—such and such an incident or such and such a neighbor—and, as if she were sewing, continually running on, thread by thread, she moved away from her initial pattern and included in her warp and weft a whole skeinful of people and stories that filled her mind, and a long time later, several hours if we let her go on, she would come full circle and return to the starting point. Extraordinary. Delirium is one of the ways of tolerating anxiety.

Spells

"There are a lot of them" is a sentence often uttered by exorcists. The most striking scene in the film *Paranormal Activity* is when the exorcist is overpowered at the threshold of the door by a huge wave of demonic activity.[25] He politely apologizes for not being able to come in. He abandons the young couple to their horror. This scene terrifies me: the courteous manner of the specialist, his remorseful impotence, his fear when he should be banishing others' fear. "There are a lot of them" are also the words that a Basque gypsy (an *erromintxela*), a bric-a-brac dealer, said to me when he came to rummage through the basement of my childhood home.

Above the bed in my bedroom-office is a large photo by Charles Fréger of an *ainara*, a swallow. It's what Basque people called the children who were sent overseas to escape the civil war after the horror of Gernika. Large tags with their names and addresses were hung around the necks of the children—eight-year-olds, ten-year-olds—sent to Colombia, Uruguay, Patagonia, Florida, Nevada, Idaho. The nickname was full of hope: swallows come back at springtime. Migration requires the courage of birds.[26]

"No one could sleep with a photo like that above them," laughs my son.

Charles Fréger, *La Suite basque, Exiliados* (The Basque
suite, the exiled), 2016

On the wall of my bedroom there is also a magic scroll,
about two meters long, that I brought back from Lalibela,
Ethiopia, in 2007—a prayer to banish the devil, written
in Amharic.

But of all the magic I've managed to explore in my family
and in my travels, Bwiti is the strongest. A ritual, a
philosophy, a traditional medicine, a culture, it origi-
nated in Gabon, in the forest around the Gulf of Guinea,
in a little tree called the iboga. Lethal in high doses, the

Detail: Saint Michael unsheathing his sword

hallucinogenic iboga plunges hopeful initiates into a lethargy, at first punctuated by vomiting. Men and women under the influence of iboga are in contact with the spirits. They enter the zone. Like Dante with Virgil, a reliable and knowled-geable guide is necessary. You have to "work with the wood," said Mallendi, the shaman who accompanied Vincent Ravalec on his initiation.[27] While "eating the wood," Ravalec relates how he met his Breton grandmother in the depths of the Gabonese forest. I've always found the possibility of reuniting with Amaxi there appealing, tempting, amusing, terrifying ... I've never dared to eat the wood.

Gabon is populated by very few human beings (probably fewer than a million), but there are a lot of other animals.

Gabon gives us a glimpse of what Earth was like before the Anthropocene: a clearing in the forest.

After four hours of travel in a canoe and a jeep, we arrived at Béti's place, at Pointe Nyonié, latitude 0, longitude 9° east. A huge mango tree dominated the camp. Béto advised us not to leave our cabins if we heard noises in the night.

It would be elephants coming to eat the mangoes. Elephants also love iboga wood. When they eat it, they wander around in a daze; and because of their size, they pose a threat.

Béti was not Gabonese, but Basque. A big, strong, older Basque guy, who asked if I was related to the rugby union player Jean Darrieussecq, known as Jeannot, a scrum-half who played internationally in the fifties and was one of the very top players in France. Jeannot was, in fact, my great-uncle, a native of Peyrehorade. Béti said, "You know the towpath on the Nive? You know the climb up to Jatxou, right after Ustaritz? That's where I'm from, where the road curves." I know the place well. The edges of the world were meeting. Basque people are travelers. They fold the world over on itself, which creates hems, hollows, new shapes.

Béti, Gabonese by adoption for forty years, had just left his wife. Things had been found under the mattress. "We've got *sorginak* in the Basque Country, but the *nganga* [spiritual healers] here are a force to be reckoned with, and if my wife is a witch, I would prefer that she didn't exercise her powers on me," Béti told me at night beneath the big mango tree, before the elephants arrived.

Keeping talismans under the bed seems to be a universal practice. In his novel *A Chronicle of Amorous Accidents*, Tadeusz Konwicki, a wonderful Polish writer born in Lithuania, tells the story of young Witek who can't sleep because of a snake skin under his mattress. In the Basque Country, the women in my family wake up with horrible dreams that are always premonitions: the feathers in Amaxi's pillow had formed the shape of crosses, or of funeral wreaths—"They're impossible to undo," she told me. But Gabon seems a particularly fertile place for spells and curses. "An entire maleficent arsenal" was found beneath the ceiling of Rosette B., "over sixty, retired from the national police force," an insomniac. "Amulets made of, among other things, a viper's head, a python's jaws, an owl's head, scorpions, six twenty-five franc pieces, a pair of underpants, two bats, live maggots, a chameleon, the shell of a bullet, a fish hook, a piece of rope with six knots and a padlock." Ever since she had moved into that house, the sixty-something-year-old "had never had a restful sleep" and, despite her Christian faith, "she stayed awake all night to see what was going to happen." The exorcist André Ella Ella—also known as "International"—diagnosed the problem and got rid of the paraphernalia in less than half an hour.[28]

Exiles

My friend Lil Sclavo in Montevideo, who is also my translator, told me about the three weeks she spent in intensive care, when she was not able to escape a dream. The dream was a ravine. The ravine was deep and dark, no trees, only crows and wind. She fought to get out of the ravine. Several years earlier, she had lost her only son, who was killed by a reckless driver. In the ravine there was no one. After the death of her son, she stayed in bed for five months. And yet she still slept at night. "That's half the solution," said the psychiatrist who was trying to help her.

I listened to Lil, my grief-stricken friend at the end of the world, and I thought of Ovid. Of his exile and of his despair at being so far from his loved ones. I loved Ovid so much that I translated his letters. It was a ravine that Ovid imagined for the separation of Orpheus and Eurydice: "They started the ascent. Everything was still, silent, steep, dark, wrapped in thick fog."[29] Ovid was exiled to Tomis, at the edge of the known world. He had "seen something he should not have seen."[30] After six months of sea and storms, abandoned on the outskirts of the Empire, where no one spoke either Greek or Latin, Ovid could no longer sleep:

> Sleep, which nourishes exhausted bodies, abandons me.
> I am on constant alert, and so are my endless anxieties.[31]

In November 2010, I was there, in Constanța, which used to be known as Tomis, the ancient city of his exile, a three-hour drive from Bucharest. It's the Danube Delta, where the ground is flat and swampy: In Ovid's world, only one boat turned up in the course of a year, if it turned up at all, with letters from Rome. I sent texts to a friend in Canada and the reply arrived within seconds, with the heartbeat *beep-beep* of the Blackberries back then: thousands of kilometers dissolved with the flick of a thumb.

There is a wretched tree or two in the open fields,
and the land is just the sea in disguise.
No bird sings, unless it has come from a forest a long way away,
giving raucous cries, drinking seawater.[32]

Ovid died in the year 18 CE, "so far from Rome on unknown shores."[33] His memory is kept alive everywhere in that part of the world. There is a statue of him in front of the mosque. But his grave has never been found. Was the coastline metamorphosed by the Danube Delta? Is Ovid, like the sleepless dead, wandering forever through the silt?

Doomed, a Roman ghost forever
flung high in the air,
wandering among Sarmatian shadows,
an eternal guest of the savage dead.[34]

In insomnia's ravine we try to collect ourselves, in vain. We look for missing bits and pieces of ourselves. It was in Tomis that Medea committed her first murder, already that of a child: "*Tomis* got its name, they say, because it was here that the sister chopped up her brother's body. Tomis comes from the Greek word for 'chop.'"[35]

> Terrified, I propped myself up on my left elbow,
> Heart thumping, and sleep abandoned me.[36]

IV

"Everyone Carries a Room About inside Them"

Everyone carries a room about inside them. This fact can be proved by means of the sense of hearing. If someone walks fast and one pricks up one's ears and listens, say at night, when everything round about is quiet, one hears, for instance, the rattling of a mirror not quite firmly fastened to the wall, or an umbrella. For we are like tree trunks in the snow. In appearance they lie smoothly and a little push should be enough to set them rolling. No, it can't be done, for they are firmly wedded to the ground. But see, even that is only appearance.

—Franz Kafka[1]

The insomniac dwells in a paradoxical bedroom: both a tomb and an entrance to other worlds. A bedroom is not simply a room. A bedroom is a world, a forest, a refuge, an abyss, a trap. The bedroom, the hollow where we retreat, has the shape of our head, of the inside of our head. It has our shape in counterrelief.

For we are like tree trunks in the snow.

We are lying there. And we don't sleep.

As sturdy as insomnia.

Abandoned room, Chernobyl Exclusion Zone, June 2018

In the *Preludes*, T. S. Eliot describes the blanket thrown from the bed "in a thousand furnished rooms," the shadows fading, the glimmer of the unforgiving dawn on the insomniac flat on her back. And it is in his own bedroom that Henri Michaux writes *Darkness Moves*: "Beneath the low ceiling of my little bedroom is my night, a deep abyss."[2]

Insomnia only ever happens in a bedroom.

Whoever complains that they can't sleep in their kitchen or in their office chair is a bit of an idiot. Of course, there's William Styron, who complains of insomnia when he can't manage a nap in the afternoon: "to the injurious sleeplessness with which I had been afflicted each night was added the insult of this afternoon insomnia, diminutive by comparison but all the more horrendous because it struck during the hours of the most intense misery."[3] Yes, it's happened that I have got out of a train in a state of despair, after not managing to sleep despite the rocking of the carriage, which usually guarantees me a bit of rest. But, really, it's when all the conditions are primed for success, in bed at night, that insomnia hits.

A Room of One's Own

Throughout history, Michelle Perrot tells us, the bedroom, a living space (the bed in the Middle Ages accommodated the whole family), shrank in size until it was nothing more than a space to retreat to, almost a hiding spot where sleep sheltered, "as rooms became bedrooms." What Virginia Woolf was advocating for in her essay *A Room of One's Own* was not a bedroom—in a bedroom a woman is quickly locked away, has too many babies, becomes a chambermaid, a maid in a chamber—no, it was definitely a room, a place for oneself. "The bedroom," says Michelle Perrot, "has lost its anthropological importance. We are no longer born at home but in the maternity ward. We no longer 'keep' to our rooms. We no longer die at home."[4] Perrot even suggests that sex allegedly left the strict confines of the bedroom in order to become more playful, but let's be careful about that claim—it seems to me that people used to fool around in wash houses just as much as they do on washing machines now.

As a child without a brother or sister, I always had my own room. Later, I shared a room in an all-girls boarding school, then my bed with various people, until I returned to the original arrangement: sleeping alone. Which means in my office. It is certainly not advisable for insomniacs to sleep and work in the same room; but at the moment, in Paris, with three children under my roof, I can scarcely have an office *and* a bedroom to myself. My husband has the marital bedroom; mine is the monastic one. In the morning we get together and discuss the endless details of our sleepless nights—fun and games at home, drama in the bedrooms.

Sleeping in separate rooms is something that provokes comment and disapproval. It is very much frowned upon.[5]

Here are photos sent in April 2020 by Rachid Hami, who was held back in Asia, of several isolation rooms during the COVID crisis.

To cut to the chase, I'll quote Michelle Perrot again: "There were [other couples] who did not share a room. [The idea of the conjugal bedroom] dissolved.... Its lack of inheritors corresponds today to that of marriage—unmarriage—in contemporary society. We have another, freer, less 'conformist' conception of a union, one that is more interested in comfort and especially in sleep. To have separate bedrooms is becoming more and more widespread and does not indicate any lack of love."[6] So there we have it.

Rereading Tarkovsky's diaries at random, I discover that my favorite filmmaker was not particularly insomniac (I'm a bit disappointed), but: "I can't sleep properly anywhere except in my own bed. And alone." Which I'm delighted about.[7]

The strategies for sleeping alone depend on the material conditions and arrangements of communal living. Ulysses managed to sleep without Penelope for a good ten years. At the end of the *Odyssey*, it's the secret of their bed that reunites them. A tree is the secret and they alone share it: Ulysses fashioned their bed from an olive tree that was cut but not uprooted. Love and sleep, sex and dreams spring forth from the stump of the tree, at the roots of Western literature.

In her novel *The Other One*, Colette justifies the practice of having a bedroom of one's own by having a threesome arrangement. The mistress has the guest bedroom, while for the first time the wife "during sleepless nights ... longed for a room where she could have slept or lain awake alone." Earlier, the married couple had invented a special piece of furniture: two beds side by side, the big marital bed for the bulky husband, and the little bed for the wife, the whole thing encased in a single frame of "English woodwork, of the Bing period."[8]

In the enigmatic book *The Yellow Wallpaper* by Charlotte Perkins Gilman, the narrator suffers from "nervous troubles" after the birth of her baby. She is prescribed rest, walks, substantial meals, and is, of course, forbidden to write. She wants to sleep in the pretty room downstairs, but her husband (who is never there) reminds her that there is not enough room for two beds, nor is there an adjoining bedroom he can retire to, whereas upstairs, in the enormous room with yellow wallpaper, they can be together. The paper has been stripped off, as if by claws, in patches all over the room, and there are patterns, shapes, and scenes of a crouching woman creeping around, as if trying to escape—at one point the narrator has to get out of bed and touch the paper to see if it is moving. Insomnia becomes her realm, insomnia becomes her madness.

The female narrator in Jean Rhys's *Voyage in the Dark* tries to maintain a certain standing as a "kept woman" by favoring two-room accommodation: she is the one who decides (at least, she tries to) at what point they move into the bedroom. And she is not obliged to stay in the bed to sleep; she is not paid to do that. Rhys is a contemporary of Woolf, who also, in *A Room of One's Own*, disapproved of bedsitting rooms, those rooms in which the bed is also for sitting on—what we call "studios" these days. There has to be a door separating *one's own place* in order to decide for oneself.[9]

In *The Unbearable Lightness of Being* by Milan Kundera, Tomas can't bear sleeping at the homes of his mistresses. Until he meets Tereza. Then he understands that there are two passions in life: making love and sleeping, passions that never connect.

Samuel Beckett and Suzanne Dechevaux-Dumesnil apparently shared a bedroom but had separate beds, then separate bedrooms once they had more money and more square meters.[10] The same went for Simone de Beauvoir and Jean-Paul Sartre, who had separate rooms in the Hotel Mistral in Montparnasse.

In the only interview Simone Boué, Cioran's wife, ever granted, she explains that their living quarters "were so small that we thought we'd end up killing each other. And Cioran, who used to get up or go to bed at any time of day or night, understood that we wouldn't last the distance." In the tiny attic above their bedroom, he created a room: "He bolted down some hardboard planks as fast

Dans cet hôtel ont habité, entre 1937 et 1939, puis à diverses reprises durant la guerre

SIMONE de BEAUVOIR
(1908-1986)

JEAN-PAUL SARTRE
(1905-1980)

"Je trichais quand je disais: on ne fait qu'un. Entre deux individus, l'harmonie n'est jamais donnée, elle doit indéfiniment se conquérir."
(S . de BEAUVOIR, La Force de l'Age)

"Mais il est une chose qui ne change point, ni ne peut changer, c'est que quoi qu'il arrive et quoi que je devienne je le deviendrai avec vous."
(J.P. SARTRE, Lettres au Castor)

Soucieux de préserver leur liberté mutuelle, ils occupaient à l'hôtel deux chambres séparées dominant le cimetière du Montparnasse où la mort les a réunis.

Association la Mémoire des Lieux

Plaque at the entrance of the Mistral Hotel, in the fourteenth arrondissement in Paris, where they slept in different rooms. (In the Montparnasse Cemetery, their tombs are also separate.)

as he could, slapdash." The highlight of this interview about insomnia is when she describes how the two night owls were forced to sleep in a municipal campground: "It was horrific."[11] The secret to successful insomnia is to sleep alone and flee any close contact, absolutely avoid others.

Let's clarify the idea of living as a couple: Beckett and Cioran are always presented as two loners, but their wives, Suzanne Dechevaux-Dumesnil and Simone Boué, were with them all through their lives. As was the case with their friend Giacometti and his wife, Annette Arm. "I owe everything to Suzanne," confided Beckett to his biographer a few weeks before his death. James Knowlson describes her admiringly as making sure that Beckett was "pestered as little as possible by unnecessary domestic chores and protecting him, as often as he allowed her, from unwelcome intrusions." It's hard to think of something comparable when it comes to women writers, assuming women writers would want this model—a Céleste Albaret free of charge. I'm thinking of the Stepford wives, those splendid housewives in Ira Levin's science-fiction novel, full of enthusiasm for domestic activities, and who don't need to sleep: robots.

A Bed of One's Own

"I am promised that cornerstone of every apartment—a bed, but not before a week," wrote Beckett when he moved into a studio on rue de Vaugirard after meeting Suzanne. The Joyces lent him "a shabby settee" that Beckett "kept very proudly for many years." Beckett's characters rarely sleep in proper beds; more often it's on the ground or on benches or in various receptacles. During the 1940 Exodus, Suzanne and Beckett slept on the floor and once on a park bench: "a horrible experience," he declared afterward, without dwelling on it any further.

Assuming one has a bed of one's own, shared or not, a bed with all the bedding assembled—bed base, mattress, linen, pillows, bolsters, quilts, bedside tables, bedside lights, a baldachin, et cetera—is still not for sleeping.

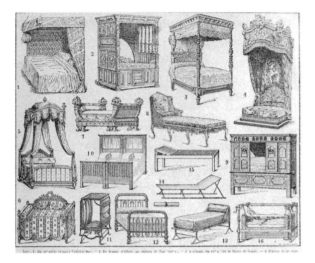

"Bed," *Larousse Universel*, an encyclopedia in two volumes, published under the direction of Claude Augé in 1922

When it comes to beds, insomniacs are the experts. Soft areas measuring from two to four square meters, beds are problematic. They accommodate the sweetest idleness or the gloomiest melancholy. For the connoisseur Xavier de Maistre, "It is here that during one half of a lifetime we forget the annoyances of the other half." He "recommend[s] every man to have, if possible, a bed with rose and white furniture.... Rose and white are two colors that are consecrated to pleasure."[12] But Maistre wasn't an insomniac; insomniacs only have one life, alas unending, not two halves of a life. "Beds were created for suffering and for pleasure," said Violette Leduc, exasperated by the excellent nocturnal health of her female lover and of her husband. "Since your sleep is stronger than my hate, I'll leave you with it, but go and hang out in the trees, lie down on the roof tops, bend over against the walls, lie back on the fountains."[13] In other words, leave the bed to the insomniacs.

Some people turn their beds into islands where they can forget everything. A raft on which to float during the storm. Franz Hessel, the Jules from Henri-Pierre Roché's 1953 novel *Jules and Jim* and the father of the famous Stéphane Hessel, called his bed "the Green Meadow."[14] He spent most of his time there. A bed is also a cubby-house, and a cubby-house recalls childhood, a refuge from the world, a magical place of one's own: *click, lock*, it's my place.

A cubby-house built by children during the lockdown, Paris, April 2020 (photo by Nelly Blumenthal). The police were informed about the construction (as well as Nelly's laundry, drying across the street). Nothing allowed on buildings! The children had to take it down.

Georges Perec observes that the bed is the only piece of furniture a law-enforcement officer does not have the right to seize. A frustrated clinophile (the technical term for someone who suffers from a love of beds; *clinophilia*, the tendency to remain in a prone position without sleeping for pronged periods of time), he is sorry not to be able to spend every day in bed.[15] In *A Man Asleep*, Perec describes this complete renunciation of all action: "and now you are well and truly a prisoner inside the pillow where it is so hot and dark that you are wondering, not without a degree of anxiety, how you are going to go about extricating yourself."[16]

Except for periods of hyperactive travel, I have spent years in my bed. Some of this time—almost two years in all—was in the first decade of the third millennium, when I had to remain lying down during four pregnancies considered by doctors to be "pathological." So the father of my children bought a king-size bed, hoping, with the optimism of daytime, that the size of it would allow us to sleep together. Once failure had been confirmed, I boarded and investigated those four square meters as if I was the captain of a flagship. You can write well in bed, and read even better, you can give birth to babies, breastfeed extremely well, and eat there despite a few crumbs, you can have a great time playing with young children, you can make telephone calls there, and enjoy complete physical relaxation (despite often getting a stiff neck); it's a marvelous place to watch films, to daydream as much as you like, there's no housework or ironing to do there. You can also get extremely depressed there. When you're in bed all day long, the flagship sinks. And when you start drinking there, it's all over. Smoking in bed is dangerous. Drinking in bed is a killer.

"Life, life, that's life / I prefer to stay in bed / Pass me a glass of whisky," sings Brigitte Fontaine.[17]

Born after a dead child (dead and not laid to rest well at all), I lack a bit of solid ground beneath me. Thanks to the birth of my three children, I have been able to step over graves. But when panic rises, enough to send me to bed, I drown: it's the temptation of the abyss. It would be better if I lay on the floor, or on the grass, or on the ground. A degree of strength comes from the horizontal plane: the hard floor, the living grass, the stability of the ground all provide hope of being able to get up again. To hang on.

Henri Michaux:

> Lying down
> lying down
> lying down in order to know
> in order to review, to confer, to decree
> to report

to undo, for tomorrow
for the sprite, for the sphere, for the waters, for the
    gesture from your innermost soul
a reclining Pharaoh
lying down.[18]

I became a psychoanalyst in order to cure myself of my clinophilia. You have to be there for the *other*, greet them standing up, and elegantly dressed if possible. Not in pajamas. My patients got me out of bed. "My patients look after me," said Winnicott.

Marcel Proust's bed (Musée Carnavalet, Paris)

Clinophiles have their king, and that king is of course Proust, heir to his aunt Léonie, she who spent her life in "complete inertia."[19] And the prince of clinophiles is Oblomov, the eponymous hero of Ivan Goncharov's novel. Saint Petersburg, 1859: Oblomov considers that his day is busy enough if his servant has managed to get him dressed around the middle of the afternoon. In love, but not lovestruck, he's a capricious lover who never leaves his couch. *Oblomovism* has become a word to describe that sort of life—preferring to remain lying down, no song and dance about anything, a long, cozy suicide, no speeches, no outrage.

Beyond the edge of the bed, there is time. Time is risk; the flow of time represents possibility. The mattress demarcates the sacred zone of oblivion, and the sheets have tucked in the whole world. Day and night no longer exist. Cioran, June 29, 1972: "More than half the day in bed. Impossible to insert myself into time."[20] Even extending your hand is to risk being snapped by crocodile time; it's risking living and dying.

The young female orphan in *Voyage in the Dark*: "It's funny when you feel as if you don't want anything more in your life except to sleep, or else to lie without moving. That's when you can hear time sliding past you, like water running."[21]

Alix Cléo Roubaud prefers the railway metaphor: "There could be a sign on the edge of a bed: *è pericoloso sporgersi.*"[22] *It is dangerous to lean out.* This sign used to be in every European train carriage, in several languages. Yes, it is dangerous to stretch your wings and jump, go off the rails. It's dangerous, very dangerous, to leave one's bed, to enter the *ruelle*, the "little street" between the bed and the wall. But there's no way the bed-lover is going there.

In *Seven*, David Fincher's 1995 film about the seven deadly sins, a clinophile is punished for his laziness by being tied to his bed—until he dies. But I don't know any lazy insomniacs. I only know exhausted insomniacs. Insomniacs stay in bed in order to sleep, and don't sleep. They are desperately in search of sleep time, time that is always lost.

Not Too Much Furniture of One's Own

"Be careful! Beds absorb more energy than any other item of furniture, because we spend at least a third of our life there and because while we're asleep we release tension."[23] Feng shui is a Chinese practical philosophy that promotes the circulation of energy in the spaces we occupy. Linked to the balance of yin and yang, the orientation of beds is crucial, and feng shui swears by wooden beds. It seems that a deep, hibernatory connection exists universally in the plant kingdom between trees and sleep.

"For high quality sleep, the ideal would be to have nothing but a bed in your bedroom! Anything in your energy field affects the quality of your sleep, so resist the temptation to stash junk under your bed. If you have one of those beds with drawers underneath, the best things to keep in there are clean bed linens, towels, or clothing."[24] As for mezzanine beds, feng shui doesn't seem to consider them. "You must not take work to bed, or put a desk in the bedroom, because the mind will not be able to detach itself from what it was focused on and will wake even more tired than when you went to bed."[25] Sensible advice given to me by the completely Western psychiatrist who tried to improve my sleep (more on this saintly woman later).

In the course of writing some of my novels, I've talked with several real-estate agents. Many of them were interested in feng shui or its Western equivalents, the energies of living spaces. Many also believed in "the memory of walls": how places can be permeated by violent deaths. One particular apartment in Paris, where the serial killer Guy Georges assassinated one of his victims, turned out to be so haunted that no one ever managed to sleep there. Like my grandmother, these agents are not lying, but I have difficulty believing them. I pace up and down with them in this zone of the unseen, which is also the zone of insomnia.

In my childhood home, I avoid sleeping alone. Year after year, for seven years, I emptied the cluttered basement, layer after layer of family junk, hoping to chase away the ghosts—or what, meet them? One of the key points of feng shui is that our houses are too full: bric-a-brac is exhausting. All its presence does is accumulate dust and deceive us with shadows; it drains our energy. All that *filling up our dresser drawers* prevents us from sleeping.[26] Declutter, toss out, clear out. Breathe, sleep. Someone should write *The Defurnisher*.

According to the sociologist Razmig Keucheyan, a German person possesses on average ten thousand objects.[27]

When it comes to Japan, Marie Kondo, the superstar of tidying up and decluttering, observed that her clients kept on average 160 tops in their cupboards: jumpers, T-shirts, cardigans, et cetera.[28] From the US, an overview of all the objects owned by John D. Freyer is available in his project *Allmylifeforsale*: this young artist from Iowa got rid of everything on eBay.[29]

Accumulate. Solidify. Objects are death, all objects, whether tidy (everything in order) or untidy (no one will find me in the pile). Furniture immobilizes—nothing can happen. When we walk in the midst of plants and animals we are moving among living things, we are part of them. When we are packed in the midst of objects, our surroundings are dead, and we are part of them, nailed down by inertness between the planks of insomnia.

The bourgeois interior, said Walter Benjamin, "forces its inhabitants to take on as many habits as they can." Habit and habitation have the same etymology, from the Latin *habere*, "to possess." Deprived of all means of subsistence when he left Germany, Benjamin was taken in by an older female friend and her daughter; he describes "the almost immemorial feeling of bourgeois security that emanated from these rooms.… [Their furnishings] attached themselves to the sauntering passage of years and days, entrusting their future to the durability of their material alone." In the middle of this "species of things … so wholly convinced of itself and its permanence … death was not provided for … that is why [the rooms] were so cozy by day, and by night the theater of our most oppressive dreams."[30]

The obsession with excess haunts all European literature, because it is inextricably linked with the bourgeoisie. In *Woodcutters*, Thomas Bernhard's hatred for a fossilized Vienna is spewed out in his loathing for bric-a-brac; and it is because of all this old junk that the pianist in *The Loser*, drowning in furniture and "almost killed finally by insomnia," went so far as to give away his piano: "I said to myself, *no more piano*."[31]

In Beckett's story "First Love," the narrator squats in a room at his prostitute friend's place: "I surveyed the room with horror. Such density of furniture defeats imagination." He begins pushing the furniture through the door to the corridor, which has the advantage of blocking the door. "I suddenly rose and changed the position of the sofa, that is to say turned it round so that the back, hitherto against the wall, was now on the outside and consequently the front, or way in, on the inside. Then I climbed back, like a dog into its basket."[32] So now he can sleep.

Céleste Albaret, too, lamented the clutter in Monsieur Proust's bedroom. She surmised that it was harmful for his breathing and for his peace of mind. "Much of the furniture which he'd inherited from his parents and, through his mother, from Uncle Louis, had been sold—there had been far too much of it. But even after the rest had been divided up between him and his brother, M. Proust still found himself with more furniture than he knew what to do with."[33] Every room in his apartment was groaning beneath chests of drawers, wardrobes, family mementos, in duplicate, triplicate, each generation piling up on top of Marcel. The only space for Céleste to move about in was in front of his bed. Barricaded like that, Proust resembles the besieged creature in one of Kafka's last works, the short story "The Burrow." Proust died in November 1922, Kafka in June 1924, leaving "The Burrow" unfinished.

Gilles Barbier, *Le Terrier* (The burrow), 2005

Hotel Rooms

Sometimes, by chance, I've fallen asleep in hotel rooms, as if travel had disconnected me from myself. The furnishings, often neutral, sometimes bewildering; a different view from the window; jetlag's huge shifts in time—these new circumstances allowed me to dump everything with my suitcases and become, in the space of one night, someone else.

Like many traveling writers, I've been obsessed with photographing the rooms where my books have led me.[34] But you can't just leave insomnia behind. It's not enough to *deterritorialize* oneself, to use that infuriating verb coined by the critical theorists Deleuze and Guattari. Giving insomnia the slip requires different strategies from those of abandoning a dog that has, by chance, been tricked. Insomnia waits, crouched on the threshold. It is unfortunately transportable and, once the initial disorientation has passed, it follows you everywhere. An insomnia of one's own.[35]

There is a room waiting for me in this city.

It is two in the morning in Belgrade and I have had a lot to drink, but there is a room for me somewhere. I have the key in my pocket, a ripped plastic map in my hand, and I have the address. I walk. It's cold, it's raining. I'm lost.

Sky Motel, Idaho

Colin's Hotel, Jacmel, Haiti

Cabin, Hurtigruten Coastal Express, Norway

Ovidiu Hotel, Constanța, Romania

Kyoto ryokan

Béti's hut, Nyonié, Gabon

Guest room at Lil's, Montevideo

Tukul Village Hotel, Lalibela, Ethiopia

Inter Hotel Salvator, Mulhouse, France

Hotel Pigalle, Gothenburg

Mosquito net, Discover Rwanda Gisenyi Beach

Double guest room at Hayet's place, Brooklyn

President Hotel, Cairo

Metro Hotel Apartments, Odessa

Sandman Signature Hotel, Newcastle upon Tyne

Hotel New World, Wuhan

Crystal Hotel, Stockholm

Residence Zodiacus, Bari

Le Havre de Paix All Suite Hotel, Kinshasa

Grand Prince Hotel, Hiroshima

Hotel de la Gare, Montluçon, France

Britannia Hotel, Trondheim

Westin Hotel, Calgary

Liège, enemy hotel room preparing for the night duel

Etc.

No memory of the name of this hotel, Belgrade

Bulevar despota Stefana is huge and windswept. I no longer know whether I'm climbing up or down. Which way is port, which way is starboard. Which direction is the Danube flowing. Which way is the city center. I walk headfirst into the gust of wind. My room is somewhere, behind all these windows. I visualize it. The bed. The walls. The sheets. Calmness. Not asleep but in the warmth. The relief of a room. For one night, for this night of rain and wind. To have a room.

Tokyo, not the worst city to be outdoors in, probably one of the safest, but the key I was entrusted with doesn't work. I arrive by train from Narita Airport. I love Tokyo, I have women friends here, but it is one in the morning and my jetlag is terrible and the damn key doesn't work. I stare at it: an inconsequential metal object, which should be a perfect fit for the lock. There is no one in the reception of the French Institute building to greet me. And I'm hardly going to call someone in the middle of the night. I think about lying down on the doorstep. This small golden object should be able to release me into peace and safety: I push the key. I push with my whole body. Something gives way. In the morning, looking out at Tokyo from the window of my room, everything is luminous.

View from my room at the French Institute, Tokyo

Haiti, November 2018, after a lovely day out with some students. Traffic jam near the airport, riots in the city. A serious storm is flooding the road, the tires are submerged, the roof of the taxi is a drum, rain seeps in through the car doors, figures crowd around, I can't see a thing. I'm in a giant washtub, a dangerous washtub. I know my hotel is nearby, but *nearby* means mud, squalls, strangers, nighttime. We have to wait, the driver remains silent, like me. I visualize a room, the door locked; secluded, calm. When I finally arrive, the tiles on the bungalow floor are covered in a centimeter of water, but the beds, like boats, are dry. The room makes me feel as if my life has been spared.

Visa Lodge, Port-au-Prince

In Kolkata's Oberoi, the city's historic palace, I am finally curled up in bed, having signed books in bookshops, chatted with members of book clubs, met teachers, students, journalists from this magnificent cultural city; yes, I am finally in my princess bedroom. It's nighttime. The air conditioning is humming. The room is on the first floor and the picture window looks out over a little street. Three meters from me, on the other side of the double glazing, fifty or so people are standing around braziers. At first I think it must be a slum. I've just had dinner with my publisher, an important woman who is always running late thanks to the traffic jams. Before our dinner, she even gave up on taking her son to his cricket match, then with great difficulty made it to the ritzy restaurant where we were meeting. In short, she spent her day in the car, where her driver seems to live, because how could you possibly find a taxi in this crazy megalopolis, where, she was sorry to say, "Mother Teresa had done so much damage" by giving a disastrous picture of the city? Anyway, beneath my window, men and women—no children—are brushing their teeth in the gutter. They wander from one makeshift camp to another along the footpath, chatting and sharing flatbread, along with steaming drinks in paper cups. The longer I look, the less I see poverty; it's more like a scene from daily life, beneath those blue tarpaulins that serve as roofs everywhere on the planet, hung from palm trees in the street, over mats carefully swept before bedtime. Later, in my sleeplessness, I get out of bed to observe the men and women again. They are asleep, eyes shut, all of them, right there on the footpath. In the morning my publisher bursts out laughing as she explains that it is not at all a slum, but rather a quiet lane where the neighborhood traders gather to sleep. Neighborhood traders? Yes, traveling salespeople, or those whose shops are so small that they prefer to sleep in the open air and return on the weekend to their homes in the sprawling suburbs of Kolkata, impossible to reach during the week because of, yes, the traffic jams.

Midrange room, the Oberoi Grand, Kolkata

Homeless

"The right to the bedroom was practically written in the Rights of Man," writes Michelle Perrot.[36]

The word *clinic* derives from the Greek word *klinē*, "bed." The clinic is what takes place around the bed. To have a bed is to have a place. A bed assumes a bedside: the possibility that someone is keeping watch. And around this bed, there must be walls, or at least curtains, screening to avoid stares. The right to intimacy, to one's life, to a death of one's own. Beneath our windows sleep the homeless, those denied rooms. On our doorsteps roam those whom the psychiatric hospitals can no longer accept, because of the outrageous lack of beds.

"Thus upon mine unrestful couch I lie / Bathed with the dews of night, unvisited / By dreams—ah me!—for in the place of sleep / Stands Fear as my familiar," says the Watchman in Aeschylus's *Agamemnon*.[37]

Houses were invented to shelter us while we sleep, when we are at our most vulnerable. "In lying down, in curling up in a corner to sleep, we abandon ourselves to a place; qua base it becomes our refuge."[38] Like a snail in its shell, our being, during sleep, is completely gathered in this place. The well-housed insomniac does not sleep, of course, but he does his not-sleeping in the warmth of his own bed. Fitzgerald refers to his bed as a sinking vessel, destined to be shipwrecked: "So deep and warm the bed and the pillow enfolding me, letting me sink into peace, nothingness."[39] Such surrender assumes supreme confidence in one's space and time, even if it is momentary— Fitzgerald wakes almost immediately, but it is not for lack of material security. Insomnia only occurs in bedrooms, at least for those inhabitants of this planet who have a bedroom at their disposal.

For the others, those without a shelter for the very personal act that is sleeping or not-sleeping, for this state of being that is strictly one's own business, insomnia is the unremitting prolongation of misery. This particular insomnia should be called something else. Take the young homeless girl whose assassins Maigret is searching for in *Maigret and the Dead Girl*. She owns nothing, or almost nothing; anonymous, she *is* almost nothing. Evicted from her room, abandoned and destitute in public squares, she stays for a time *under* the bed of a girlfriend, in order to hide from the landlady. According to the list Maigret draws up when she dies, she leaves only a shabby dress, a toothbrush, some cheap face powder, a photograph of her father, and, yes, a vial of sleeping pills.[40]

A Bookshop in Berlin, by Françoise Frenkel, is the story of a young Jewish bookseller forced to leave occupied Germany and France and finally make a clandestine crossing into Switzerland.[41] In a voice that is assured, but as if strangled by a sob, she describes the fear that prevents her from sleeping, the rooms where she hides, the beds from which she is chased. The only trace of Frenkel after the war is a 1958 form she filled out for the indemnification of her suitcase, which was stolen as "Jewish property." Patrick Modiano, who wrote the preface for the book, lists the contents: "One coypu fur coat. One coat with an opossum collar. Two woolen dresses. A black raincoat. A dressing gown from Grünfeld's. An umbrella. A parasol. Two pairs of shoes. A handbag. An electric heat pad. An Erika portable typewriter. A Universal portable typewriter. Gloves, socks, and handkerchiefs."[42]

The possibility of sleep, rest, depends on owning something, or at least having something at your disposal. Which is no doubt what we find so heartrending about these enumerations of lost property: their loss signifies the loss of everything. Because empty burrows are not enough for us human animals.

"House," thirteenth arrondissement, Paris

In Kafka's *The Castle*, K is forever being confronted with his condition as a foreigner. "We have no use for visitors," says one inhabitant. But K is going to try to sleep here permanently. A refugee is not here for the day. An asylum seeker needs more than one night. In this final, unfinished novel, K is looking, night after night, for a room. There's no question of staying at the Castle. It's even impossible to stay at the inn: "Strangers aren't allowed into the castle without permission." Impossible to get to the right counter; no one knows what the process is. "Why did you wake me, then?" K is a good sleeper, as the first pages of the novel attest, but all these people leaning over him, telephoning to find out whether or not he has the right to stay there, and "the telephone turned out to be almost above his head"—naturally that prevents him from sleeping. In the end the villagers tolerate K and his fiancée sleeping at the school, but the couple have to change rooms as soon as classes start, and they often wake up with people staring at them.[43] It was K I saw in the bleak buildings, closed-down secondary schools, repurposed gymnasiums, in sleeping bags, lying underneath lines of T-shirts and socks hanging out to dry, as the breakfast food rations were distributed, in Paris, in Cachan (to the south of Paris), in Calais, in Grande-Synthe (a suburb of Dunkirk).

Gymnasium in Grande-Synthe, men's side, winter 2018

All those repurposed gyms, all those cities that chose to allow their citizens to go without them, because it is more important to provide shelter than to do sport, and all those mornings of waking up beneath wall bars, beneath basketball rings, beneath stares, and me, *the foreigner*, uneasy, arriving in order to leave, to write a story about it.

And how did we get from this word in the 1990s, *undocumented*, an accurate, descriptive expression, to the word *migrant* (from the verb *migrate*), which keeps those exiled people up in the air, on hold, while those who are *emigrés* (from the verb *emigrate*) can finally settle?

In February 2018, I was invited by the television program *Arte* to report on what was happening in Calais. I also had in mind my novel *Crossed Lines*. Congolese, Cameroonians, Nigerians, Sudanese, Somalis, Eritreans, Iraqis, Kurds, Syrians, Afghans—everyone I managed to talk to told me they wanted *security*. "I want the same security as you," Jacob, an Iranian Jew, told me. The same words were uttered by two Oromo Ethiopians, both called Thomas, who had fled the state of emergency declared by the ethnic group in power there. Their need for security often created a misunderstanding with the activists in Calais, those from the No Borders Network, or the young Brits from Care4Calais, who were some-times opposed to the authorities on principle, whereas the migrants I met were counting on the integrity of our police (do we know anything about the police in Eritrea?). They were anxious about their unintentional illegal status, and were all the more shocked and disappointed when the police force of a democracy turned violently against them, the weakest of all.

Alas, in *The Castle*, the son of the warden "could not, even with the best intentions, avoid disturbing K" while he slept.[44]

I was there right after the dismantling of the "Jungle." The orders were to demolish every bit of the camp. The migrants were driven out in their sleep, at their most vulnerable, in the middle of the night. During this "organized inhospitality," I saw their last place of refuge—sleeping bags—soaked in tear gas.[45]

"Habitat," between Calais and Dunkirk

Living in a place that can be easily erased. Nonplaces, non-camps, situated in a country but also outside of it, outside political geography. Places peopled with nonsubjects, at the same time detained and refused entry: nonpeople. Nonpersons. And when you are a nonperson, you non-sleep—nonsleeping is all there is.

I said to myself: Sleeping in a safe place should be a right, but so should sleeping pure and simple, sleeping through the night, the right to a nocturnal break, just like a winter break. Not to be dislodged, at least, from one's sleep. From that place of one's own that sleep should be.

In 2014, I flew direct to the departure point of the migrants' journey: Niamey, the capital of Niger, where those journeying from West Africa to cross the Sahara converge. And also the point of return, or nonreturn, because it was where those driven out of Libya and Algeria ended up—they had nothing. Not a room, not even a tarpaulin, occasionally some cardboard. Trapped in Niger, no way forward, no way back; they didn't have the fifty euros (30,000 Central African CFA francs) to return home to Cameroon, Ghana, the Ivory Coast, to the green and luxuriant Gulf of Guinea, where there was no future for them.

In Niger, a sheet of roofing metal, one meter by two, costs 3,000 francs. They're given as a dowry to girls. One

Hôtel Terminus, Niamey, 2014

night in my hotel cost the equivalent of ten sheets of
metal, a whole roof—or the price of a ticket home for
them. I was staying in what was for me relative comfort,
nervously watching the bathtub, next to which was
growing, night after night, centimeter by centimeter, a
termite mound of a beautiful ochre color, leaning against
the tiles.

Anonymous section, Calais Cemetery

In Calais the destitution of the *exodés* (the name given to them in Niger) was at the same time less severe than in Niamey—food was distributed and there were showers—but more visible. Young bodies huddled in the piles of gravel, trying to shelter from the icy wind. What's it like, sleeping in gravel, in a flimsy anorak? "What's it like" is the expression for "Hello" in Cameroon, "How's it going?"

In the evening, when I was chilled to the bone and left them, they were gracious. "You have to go back inside to get warm and rest so you're in good shape to write your novel." My room looked out over the port. Perhaps one of the guys I'd spoken with was in the belly of a truck, on one of the ferries whose lights were receding. And there I was, at four in the morning, with my Holiday Inn insomnia.

Holiday Inn Hotel, Calais

V

A World of Networks and Vines

I am the wolf
Who does not sleep
I'm not frightened of you
You are frightened of me.
—Grégoire Solotareff [1]

The provision of safe sleeping arrangements for everyone is a social indicator of the birth of the state.

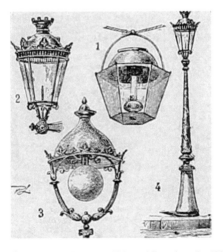

"Street lamps," *Larousse Universel Encyclopedia*, 1922

Historians such as A. Roger Ekirch describe how, little by little, public lighting and night patrols were organized first in cities, and then throughout the rest of the country.[2] Street lighting on main roads became a political initiative in the Middle Ages. It was a matter of guaranteeing that everyone could sleep safely, but also of ensuring that people slept, or at least stayed home.[3] Before the industrial revolution, night work was illegal in the majority of businesses. Every vagrant was suspicious, every female out walking was a witch or a prostitute, while the patrolling officers themselves were required to keep their eyes open. In a sense, not-sleeping was the monopoly of the state. Anyone who didn't sleep was feared or frowned upon.

Open Twenty-Four Hours

The ascendancy of electricity accelerated the streamlining of cities and metamorphosed the relationship between human beings and the night. Once Electra is domesticated, citizens can, and must, work, regardless of the position of the sun in the sky.

Jonathan Crary, in his book *24/7: Late Capitalism and the Ends of Sleep*, deciphers how capitalism has succeeded in commodifying all our basic needs: light, heat, water, food, housing, sex, and even friendship. But it still has trouble expropriating sleep. It therefore permanently illuminates the night so that the conditions under which frenetic production takes place are a form of generalized insomnia. The watchword from now on: *open twenty-four hours.*

"Illness never sleeps. Neither do we. #WithoutRespite 7000 new drugs in development." Ad for pharmaceutical companies in the Paris Métro, October 2017.

But now it is not so much light stopping us from sleeping as nonstop connectivity. "We are dictated to by the news," said Gilles Deleuze back in 1980. Drawing our attention to one conflict rather than another, to a particular human-interest story rather than a particular event—that's what constructs our "current affairs." The instruction is given using verbs intransitively: a news item will "be of interest," a banking term; we might even be "mobilized," a military term. The broadcasting and receiving of signals has become a sort of modern way of breathing, on a planet that would have to stop turning in order for us to continue our social messaging ad infinitum, without nocturnal interference.

Sleep then becomes a structural attention deficit, a systemic anomaly in humans: "Microsoft has revealed it took five hours to acknowledge lengthy disruptions affecting European customers ... because the task of informing customers relied on a US-based incident manager, who was asleep at the time." I'm reading this in April 2020, between two news stories on the coronavirus: "When incidents involve customer request failures ... we have automated tooling that starts an incident and loops in both a DRI (designated responsible individual) and what we call a PIM (primary incident manager)," explains Chad Kimes, director of engineering at Azure. "While the DRI was hard at work understanding the technical issues and looking for potential mitigations, the PIM was still asleep."[4] "To sleep" or to be "on sleep mode," the same vocabulary for humans and machines, the same requirement for alertness and efficiency: we no longer know who is automated or who should be.

Because of this injunction to be not only attentive but responsive at all times, "sleeping is for losers," according to Jonathan Crary's diagnosis. When Trump tweeted at three in the morning, he presented the image of himself as awake, alert. The strongman, with machine-like energy, is active while we're asleep. Could we imagine Big Brother sleeping?

Ad for slimming foam, "anti-cellulite in 7 nights."
Products that work at night are commonplace
in cosmetics.

And yet most of us need to sleep. Joshua Trump, an eleven-year-old American invited by his homonym to the State of the Union address, was called a hero by anti-Trump followers for having fallen asleep during the sacrosanct spiel.[5] In the popular French absurdist TV animation series *Les Shadoks* (1968–1974), on the planet Shadok, even the feet-on-top Shadoks, who stopped the planet from falling, had to sleep from time to time, "so, when they were on their backs, their feet no longer supported anything."[6]

The liberal economy burns up its human resources the way it does coal or oil. Work structures produce more and

And "the planet immediately grew deformed."
Jacques Rouxel, *Les Shadoks: Pompe à rebours*,
(Paris: Grasset, 1975).

more burnout, workers are "consumed." Vulcan, the god of work and fire, and his forge torment us even in our beds. "It seemed to him as if a heartless blacksmith, a lugubrious outrider, a cruel cyclops was working his entrails, hammering away at his fragile skeleton," wrote Paul Gadenne in "Insomnia."[7]

In the past, before the word *burnout* existed, we talked about being "overworked." The solution was to stop work temporarily. Then, under the pretext of yet another "crisis," this time the European fuel crisis of 1974, new work arrangements transformed workers into furnaces that were never turned off. Bullyish management no longer aimed at monitoring personnel but rather liquidating them. With Management and Performance Review in power, work was accompanied by analyses of work, with the paradoxical aim of increasing productivity: reports, tables, spreadsheets, activity

When my father oversaw maintenance at the foundries of Mousserolles, he was in charge of the smelting and was often woken in the night, whenever one of the machines broke down. Which did nothing for his sleep, nor, alas, for his tobacco consumption. Looking at a photo of himself at work, in Bayonne in the seventies, he told me he was "inside a continuous oven that had broken down, trying to work out the problem and how to repair it. Very unpleasant for a claustrophobic person." (Bayonne, 1970s.)

charts, logbooks, news lists, accreditations and recommendations, protocols and procedures, orientation booklets and best-practice guidelines, client files, patient records, student-assessment records, quality-assurance processes, reviews, *entrepreneurial-potential self-assessment forms ...*

On September 21, 2019, Christine Renon, the "exhausted principal" of the Méhul de Pantin school, wrote a letter addressed to the Ministry of National Education before throwing herself from the roof of her school. On the three closely written pages where she detailed the mountain of absurd tasks she was required to complete, the lists of reports on goals and objectives, "prospects" that were always in the future (and it is as if, as she wrote, she didn't know that at the end of her letter she would kill herself, as if writing it led her to this harrowing conclusion), she also notes "the prospect of having to wait to see my doctor about the cough that has prevented me from sleeping for three days."

"In the Penal Colony" is a short story written by Kafka two months after the start of World War One. A man is going to be executed. What was his wrongdoing? "He is duty bound at the stroke of each hour to stand up and salute at the door. To be sure, hardly a daunting responsibility, but a necessary one, as the man must remain alert both as a guard and servant. The captain last night wanted to confirm that the man was doing his duty. At the stroke of two he opened the door and found him rolled up and fast asleep on the floor." The rule that the condemned man has violated will be inscribed on his body by a machine: "Honor your superiors." That sentence will be etched more and more deeply into his body, until he dies.[8]

Networks and Transparencies

Stefan Zweig, two weeks after the start of World War Two: "From now on, an endless network covers the world, all day and all night." No one is alone in their bed anymore. Each individual knows that "thanks to our new methods of spreading news as it happens, we have been constantly drawn into the events of our time.... Incidents thousands of miles away came vividly before our eyes. There was no shelter, no safety from constant awareness and involvement."[9]

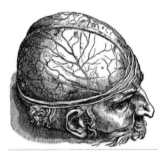

Andreas Vesalius, *De humani corporis fabrica* (*The Fabric of the Human Body*), anatomical treatise, sixteenth century

Globe on my desk

The networks crisscross our sleep, the rhizomes grow in our brains. This new environment has spread steadily, speeding up. There is no escape from the news. We are a community filled with anxiety. We are as global as bubbles. And we also like this instantaneous medium that is now so familiar. We order American-made objects that arrive in our European letterboxes, sent from addresses in China. We see them on our screens and they materialize in our apartments. *The annihilation of space by time*: Marx predicted it, Amazon enabled it. And in the mid-2000s we saw people living in Brisbane, Mumbai, Lagos, or Buenos Aires, pixelating all at the same time on

Skype videoconferences. Our still-faltering communication systems, with flickering images and intermittent audio, gave those years their old-world tone. During lockdown, the use of these apps multiplied exponentially— FaceTime, Zoom, Teams, Jami, Discord, and others. *Discordia, daughter of the night,* in Homer's words.

And in the general conversation between meridians, in the *here-and-now straightaway,* at least one of the participants will not have slept. In their time zone, the call will have cut into the time normally devoted to sleep. The call was just one of many demands hovering in the air: everything can happen everywhere and all the time.

Instead of being enhanced by the transaction, we are tormented by what is lost.

"There is less sleep in the world today," wrote Stefan Zweig.[10] There is also less of our *body,* despite the proliferation of human beings on the planet. And the body, it seems to me, is sleep. Studies remain inconclusive, with contradictory results, about whether we slept or not during lockdown.[11] When the coronavirus paralyzed Wuhan, Xiaoyu Lui, who lives in the center of the city, said in the week of January 31: "My neighborhood is almost deserted, and I am sleeping unusually well."

The writer Fang Fang, also from Wuhan, kept a blog, translations of which quickly traveled round the world.

The lights of Wuhan on a rainy night, March 17, 2018, "before"

On January 29, she confesses to sleeping until midday every day—as usual, she clarifies, but now without "blam[ing] myself." But on February 11, she adds, "for more than 20 days now, I have been relying on sleeping pills to fall asleep each night"—that is, since the beginning of lockdown.[12] Bombarded by anxiety-inducing news, by rumors and propaganda, she is also on the receiving end of violent attacks on an internet that is censured by the party and swamped by ultranationalists: her solitude is overcrowded.

Whether we're locked down or not, it's clear that, even in our bedrooms, *space is annihilated by time.* Do you have your own room? All sorts of devices surround you. Electromagnetic waves circulate. Diodes keep their eyes peeled. No matter how often you put your device on "airplane mode," on "ghost mode," on "do not disturb," the world—at your fingertips, just like in the ads—demands that you stay present. In the depths of insomnia, you go online again. Your pupils contract in the blue light of the screen. An artificial dawn. You read your text messages and comments, you look at and listen to images, you discuss, perhaps you add a comment and you *like*, you look at things that are your business and that others are perhaps making it their business to look at too.

Those born before the 1990s remember boredom. In order to live, you had to get out of your bedroom at all costs. We all know Pascal's refrain: "The sole cause of man's unhappiness is that he does not know how to stay quietly in his room."[13] How guilt-inducing. We don't want to stay in our room. The lockdowns proved that to us. And, even if we wanted to, that room no longer exists. It has become an online space, where boredom has been replaced by impatience. In the nostalgic Pascalian room, it was possible to be an isolated speck on a little-known planet. And it was possible to remain private, opaque. These days, we are summoned by planetary time; it travels through us. We are compelled to participate. Even in the bedroom, that famous *rest* is difficult to achieve.[14] Time spent in the bedroom is itself evaluated, judged, measured, approved or disapproved, according to the demands of work, communication, or health. *An hour to yourself?* It sounds like an advertisement for a leisure center or a body treatment. The walls of Virginia Woolf's marvelous *room of one's own*, that absolutely private space she dreamed of for women, have been knocked down, regardless of gender, regardless of style.

The walls, porous to the world, become as transparent as in the visionary nightmare of Yevgeny Zamyatin, Orwell's precursor. In his novel *We*, the totalitarian city is made entirely of glass. At 10:30 p.m., everyone has to sleep, blinds up (they are only lowered for authorized sexual relations). But citizen D-503 can't sleep. "I argued with myself: At night numbers must sleep; it is their duty, just as it is their duty to work in the daytime. Not sleeping at night is a criminal offense." The first symptom of rebellion in this supposedly transparent subject is insomnia. And when he doesn't sleep, he dreams, he discovers the hypnagogic state. "My bed rose and sank and rose again under me, floating along a sinusoid." "You're in a bad way! Apparently, you have developed a soul!" announces the doctor.[15]

Fifteen years later, in the Germany of the Third Reich, the psychiatrist Charlotte Beradt collected seventy-five-odd dreams in a book that became famous. Like this nightmare from a forty-five-year-old doctor: "Suddenly the walls of my room and then my apartment disappeared. I looked around and discovered to my horror that as far as the eye could see no apartment had walls anymore. Then I heard a loudspeaker boom, 'According to the decree of the 17th of this month on the Abolition of Walls.'"[16]

A forest full of supposedly wild beasts surrounds the glass city in *We*. A wall protects the city from all that disgusting freedom. D-503 is going to make a break for the forest.

Insomnia and Forests

During the expansion of the modern world, the forest has become a place of refuge and a place to avoid. You escape to the woods and you get lost in the woods. The forest is a world of fairies and of danger, a glade outside time, a maze. And in this expedition beyond the walls, perhaps a different type of sleep awaits us, plantlike.

We know about the sleep of trees. As children we join in autumn rituals. The sap descends, the leaves fall, we collect them and play in the dancing wind. Childhood amounts to ten autumns. If winter is the trees' nighttime, in spring they wake from their vertical sleep. They're not being reborn. Children understand that quickly enough. A tree without leaves is not a dead tree, but a tree that is sleeping, waiting quietly for winter to pass. In equatorial

Forest in the Andes, on the Argentina-Chile border, a day's hike from El Bolson. Old growth forests look like parks.

forests, trees are insomniacs. Their leaves grow incessantly and fall when they fade, constantly regrowing in all that green wakefulness. We cut down these thousand-year-old forests and insomnia spreads. The trees release it throughout the world like an evil gas, and we are being asphyxiated.

A farmed, fifty-year-old spruce tree, a Christmas tree that was planted then sacrificed because it blocked the view

One of our years is the equivalent of a day in the life of a tree. A growth ring equates to one night in a tree's life.

The Chernobyl Exclusion Zone, June 2018: the forest is everywhere. The trees have a sci-fi exuberance about them. Their roots raise staircases and make walls collapse. New growth is shooting through what is left of the asphalt.

Semicollapsed bleachers open onto foliage.
The Pripyat football field became a forest.

There are birds everywhere. Foxes have the run of the place. Bears and wolves have returned from Belarus. I have that forgotten feeling of brushing away swarms of little flying creatures from my face. Enormous and *normal* swarms of insects. Clouds of dragonflies. Airborne plankton.

Childhood memories of being in the country, the humming noises, and those droves of creatures in the grass, in the trees, on silken threads, in webs, in cocoons. Life. A few steps to one side—the curiosity of *Homo sapiens sapiens* is like that of a fox—and our dosimeters start beeping like crazy: invisible "spillages." Especially under houses, in the dry grass. The radioactivity ran off the roofs that were hosed down after the 1986 catastrophe.

In 2020, for the whole of the month of April, historically dry because of climate change, this forest burned, exposing Ukrainian firemen to the double danger of fire and radioactivity, while the rest of the world, locked down by coronavirus, remained relatively indifferent.

(I'm trying to imagine the effect that sentence, out of science fiction, would have had on me as a child.)

"I suffered from insomnia and had lost my zest for life." In his *Journal Written at Night*, the Polish writer Gustaw Herling-Grudziński invents a dystopia where an insurance agent, "in charge of the forestry department," makes an annual trip to the Sistine Chapel to revitalize his soul; but now that the cigarette lighter has been invented, the forests go up in flames. Everyone stays up all night on Saint Peter's Square. A whole new group of people set up camp and chant around small fires. Next the Sistine Chapel burns down.[17]

The first lines of *The Divine Comedy*, illustrated by Gustave Doré

The forest has been with us forever, ever since we became that species with upright posture. And before we stood up, we were no doubt hanging on by the first human hands. The opening of *The Divine Comedy*: "In the middle of our life's journey, I found myself in a dark wood, where the straight way was lost." Even Dante descended from the apes. In line 11, he has no idea how he entered the *dark wood*, because he was "full of sleep"; in line 28, he rests a bit; in line 29, he continues his descent (this forest is a ravine); in the next lines, all sorts of animals bar his way; in line 62, Virgil appears: Phew, here's the guide. The whole journey is nothing more than a long negotiation between sudden sleeps and unforgiving insomnia.[18]

In the middle of my life's journey, from what I could estimate as the forty-something I was, I was blocked two-thirds of the way through writing a novel. For the readers who may be interested, it was precisely at the sentence: "And which seer could read her future, when her entrails were uncoiled in the labyrinth?"[19] Without a seer on hand, I had no choice; I had to follow my characters where they took me: into the forest. The real one. The ancient, virgin forest that had grown without the presence of human beings. I had to enter that forest, I who had always stayed back cautiously on the edge.

Unable to talk about it with Virgil, I asked the writer Jean Rolin. Gabon was expensive. Of course, there was always the Democratic Republic of Congo, what used to be Zaire, but Jean recommended Cameroon—slightly fewer weapons in circulation, slightly less chaos. In Southern Cameroon, it's "the same forest, the Congo Basin." The names were the stuff of dreams. I was already traveling via satellite images. To the south of the Sanaga River stretched an immense area that looked attractive, empty. Kalliopi

Google Earth screenshot taken in 2012. The Campo Ma'an zone, sprinkled with mist, was as white as it was green.

Ango-Ela, another beautiful name, advised me to go to Campo Ma'an, "because the track to Dja is impassable at the moment." A country of potholes and big trees appeared in my mind while I talked to her on the phone, leaning back on my pillows. I remember her practical, impatient instructions: I was setting off with no idea about the seasons, the rain, anything.

The bitumen road from Yaounde to Kribi was already in a bad state, and from the Lobé Falls on it was rutted and muddy. The trees were closing in around us. The forest was growing, higher and higher, at the jolting speed of the car. I let myself be lulled by the air conditioning and the sound system playing great Congolese rumba, chosen by Djibrill, the driver recommended to me because I couldn't have managed a four-wheel drive in the forest. From the radio: "We presented the problem, we did not present the solution," *tiditadada tiditadada* ... Insomniacs tend to nod off in cars, and I was a victim of the common feminine illusion of placing oneself somnambulistically under the wing of whichever man was driving. But Djibrill was a city person like me and it was the first time—he finally told me—that he had ventured into the forest. With a violent bang, the floor of our four-wheel drive struck the ground and we crashed into a hole.

I opened the door and the air-conditioning bubble was destroyed. The forest loomed above me. The heat was as overwhelming as the noises—creaking, whistling, cries. A line of stars shone between two high black walls split open by the strip of sky. I was in another space, like a cosmonaut bursting out of a space shuttle. The universal joint was broken. Djibrill couldn't repair it. He couldn't make a call—there was no network. That was when I sensed his terror. At night the forest is inhabited by spirits. I was immune to that particular fear (rightly or wrongly): my ghosts lived in the forests of the Basque Country. I had a whole lot of other fears. Djibrill retreated into the shelter of the car. Feeling useless, I preferred to stay outside, watching all the strangeness.

Two men burst out of the forest. In rags, reasonably drunk, and armed with machetes. Later I found out that everyone (except Djibrill and me) carries a machete in the forest, which did not bode well when it came to the

unpredictable behavior of the locals. With a little bit of French and a lot of gestures, they convinced us to push the car off the track. Not that the traffic was heavy, of course. But to hide it. We managed to more or less conceal it beneath the trees, and we covered the rest of it with palm fronds that the obliging woodsmen cut for us—with, as it happens, their machetes. I felt as if I was camouflaging an enormous pile of dollar notes that was going to be slashed to bits once our fate had been similarly settled. But *Homo sapiens sapiens*, in adversity, tends to do any old thing rather than nothing.

Two headlights broke through the dense trees. It was a pickup truck coming from Campo Ma'an. They were on a mission to find the tourist woman; the pile of dollar notes was me, and that night Virgil's name was Monsieur Sock, the chief ranger.

At V&T's hostel in Campo Ma'an, two large, scantily dressed women, Valérianne and Toussainte, were fanning themselves on a vinyl couch in a small living room that opened onto the forest. They handed me my key without a word, perhaps because I had arrived a lot later than expected, but forest time, I was to learn, has nothing to do with human time. The room was clean, the floor made of beaten earth. A toilet stood in pride of place in a tiled corner, no running water, but a bucket. The bed was immaculate, square, with nylon sheets that smelt of bleach. Another perfectly ironed sheet, same fabric and same smell, served as a towel. Djibrill insisted on sleeping elsewhere. Later I found out that V&T's was too expensive for him.

My dinner consisted of Kit Kat chocolate bars and the rest of my mineral water. I placed my last bars, still wrapped up, on the Castrol oil drum that served as a bedside table, along with a book, my toothbrush, and a bottle of water sterilized with purification tablets. I pulled on long pajamas to deter bugs, and I burrowed under the sheet. I could hear the sounds of a football match coming from the living room, along with gurgles, cries, screeching, and chattering from the forest. Slightly fewer mosquitoes than in Yaoundé. But impossible to sleep. I don't sleep in my bed in my bedroom in my apartment in my city, so how am I going to sleep at V&T's in the forest?

After a while I put my clothes back on. I went out onto the patio with my book. It was midnight, in the depths of the twelve hours of equatorial night. In the living room, two big blokes were chatting with V&T while keeping an eye on the match.

I was counting on the fresh air, on reading or listening to the call of the forest or what have you, in order to "come back down," a concept that is very familiar to insomniacs. I was so flabbergasted to be there, and so relieved to have found a bed, that I wasn't sleeping

The air was certainly not fresh. But, yes, the forest was calling me. I was euphoric. As I write these lines, seven years later, in winter, in my Parisian office from where I see the courtyards of mostly Haussmann buildings, a big bare plane tree, and the roof of a modern building that has been "greened"—so, thousands of kilometer-years from that night at V&T's—I can recall the feel of the plastic chair, the vast humid heat, the motionless air, the vibration of the insects, the pitch-black forest whose closest leaves were almost touching me. I rediscover my anticipation of what the day would bring. I am in a space capsule of unchanging time, I am in the hyperawareness of insomnia. And yet I'm losing my memory because of barbiturates.

"To lose oneself in a city—as one loses oneself in a forest—that calls for quite a different schooling," wrote Walter Benjamin.[20]

Activities insomniacs resort to: reading or walking. Or drinking, which doesn't exclude the first two options.

Reading: a single light bulb hung at the entrance, illuminating both the living room and the patio. By "patio" I mean a small awning above the chair I was sitting in. A large insect was whirling loudly around the bulb, and it took all my dignity not to cause a scene, under the gaze of the four pairs of eyes trained on me from the living room.

Walking: there were only two possibilities—toward the top of the track, which was plunged in darkness but where I could make out a building painted in bright yellow (I found out the following day that it doubled as the town hall and the forest ranger's office); or toward the bottom of the track, where the music was coming from, and where a red light was shining and, farther along, some fairy lights. (Later on I visited these neighborhoods, known as Washington and Paris-Soir.)

Drinking: the music was coming from one of those little bars they call *maquis* everywhere in francophone Africa. The most popular of them, I found out the next day, had a magnificent name, the Straight Way. Perhaps less a quote from *The Divine Comedy* (*ma chi lo sa?*) than a way of snubbing their nose at the omnipresent Bible, an homage to our drunken staggering, and to the forest in our minds ...

"Where are you going?" said one of the big blokes. "That is not high-quality place for you. You will have the problem." He continued, "Here is like the city of the gold diggers. Here is like kung fu." The hope of getting a nighttime beer in Campo Ma'an vanished.

I took a sleeping pill, the ultimate and too frequently used recourse of insomniacs, and immediately sank into the slippery sheets.

A huge racket woke me up. The Castrol oil drum was clanging like a bell. In the glow from my Blackberry, a swarm of mice was scurrying over my Kit Kats. I leapt up. All the mice disappeared at once. I put the rest of the chocolate in a sealed bag and rubbed my hands compulsively with hand sanitizer. And went straight back to sleep.

Like prisoners released in sleep,
To roam the forests green.[21]

Sleeping tablets last for several hours. Or else—I can't remember—perhaps I took another one.

When I woke up next morning at dawn, I was sluggish. V&T's backed onto a sinister plantation of rubber trees, rows of them lined up like a bad dream. There you go, I said to myself, while my insomnia thrives, they're deforesting. I entered the forest with Siméon and Parfait, one very tall, the other very short. Siméon scythes. Parfait guides. Siméon tells me later that he's incapable of finding his way in this forest despite years of "habituation." Parfait is one of the Bagyeli people; no one uses the pejorative word *pygmy*. I try to wake up amid the clouds of little bees, as bits of undergrowth snag on me from all sides. We reach a track. It's an elephant's track. In 2013, there are still elephants here, little forest elephants. Our path clears. And all of a sudden we are in a park. The dream continues. The trunks form the pillars of a nave. It's virgin forest. Intact. The ground is open, clear. We walk around a single tree for a long time. The kapok trees grow large waves of bark. I can stand upright between two folds. The sky is green. The solidity of these trees, their lofty indifference to mammals: I see them, they don't see me. But I sense that they sense me; our presence has been detected. They hold up another sky. We walk along, minuscule and silent.

Siméon at the campsite

Siméon Zeng Mengue is armed with an old MAS-36 rifle, a machete, and a dagger. I find him very sexy. He looks after everything, lugging around the tent, the camping stove, the food, the pots and pans, and why not a sedan chair while we're at it? I had to insist on carrying my backpack myself. He tells me that my three-day trek represents two months of a salary the Cameroon government has not paid him for two years.

Parfait is not carrying anything and doesn't seem to need anything. He negotiated his own salary with Siméon. He drinks from the vines he cuts; it's transparent water, water from a dream. Siméon lets me taste it: if the color green has a taste, this is it. Parfait also drinks out of strange little plastic sachets. The Bagyeli are part of the Baka tribes of hunter-gatherers, who are Indigenous to the forest. There are only a few thousand of them left. Capitalist time has destroyed the Bakas' space.[22]

Parfait is furious because "women don't go into the forest." A bit annoyed, Siméon translates. "Women contaminate the forest." Parfait is on strike, we're not going any further. As a white person, I am imposing my presence by trampling on his traditions; as a woman, I'm subjected to universal exclusion and insult. Parfait lies down under a tree. He falls asleep immediately. Like a log. He is dead drunk. Siméon seems resigned to both the alcoholism of the guide and the naivety of his female client. Since the start of our expedition, Parfait has been sucking on gin sachets that I assumed were water pouches.

There in the forest populated by rare animals and any number of plants, I contemplate Parfait huddled in his drunkenness. The resistance posed by his sleep is extraordinarily effective.

In the evening we camp on the bank of a river. The fire goes out as soon as Siméon stops tending it. This forest is made of water rising toward the sky. The air we're breathing is a purée of warm water and oxygen. And I am a little power plant of thoughts.

I can't take the forest into myself. It is around me and I'm breathing it. Disappearance is a possibility. If Parfait abandoned us for good, the forest couldn't care less that we'd lost our way. Couldn't care less about the middle of our life's journey. Or our two legs, our hands, our brain, our upright posture: the forest raises its trunks above our heads. The sun's path is concealed. There are no stars. Walking is a series of moments: one step, another step. Here, yes, the straight way is lost.

Siméon pitches the tent for me. The two men, one very tall and one very short, get settled outside on mats. "Under the stars" doesn't apply here: *under the canopy*, perhaps. I'm suffocating beneath my cloth roof. I haul myself out of the tent. Siméon wakes up and helps me to set up my mat outside. I hear him go back to sleep instantly.

I think about Mary Kingsley, the English explorer in crinoline. In her journal she describes how she manages to sleep no matter what is happening around her: "I dash under the mosquito bar and sleep, lulled by their shrill yells of baffled rage." Often not discovering until morning that scorpions had been trapped there too. During long trips in dugout canoes, she sleeps deeply, sitting up, her hands clasped between her knees because of the crocodiles.[23]

There are those who sleep, and then there are the others. That's all there is to it.

I'm lying on my mat, wrapped in my sleeping bag. Only my nose poking out. I don't know if tarantulas and centipedes are nocturnal. They must be. There are no mosquitoes but there are things flying around. Any yet I'm not worried.

But I'm not asleep.

The river carves a narrow opening of sky between the foliage. I see a few stars, moving like clouds. Sections of the forest light up. Shifting trees. Fluorescent ghosts. Floating swarms of insects—fireflies, glowing intermittently. I grab my Blackberry to film the flickering night. I can only see blackness and the opening between the leaves. But I can hear them.[24] The forest is a hypnagogic zone.

I have a choice between Donormyl, Stilnox, and Lexomil: I brought all three in my backpack. Along with earplugs and a toothbrush. And sunscreen too, stupidly, for the days spent completely shrouded by trees.

When those close to me worry about what they call my "fearlessness," I don't tell them that my insomnia is what is holding me back. In order to keep going, I have to knock myself out.

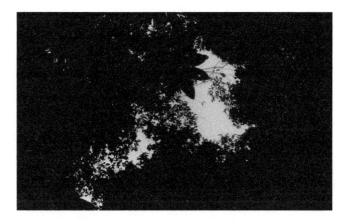

I opted for the Donormyl, although it gives me a dry throat and makes me prone to snoring. I stuck the earplugs in and set the alarm on my Blackberry for just before dawn, so that Siméon wouldn't have to shake me awake.

He and Parfait were hilarious as we ate out of our mess tins at breakfast: apparently, I had snored louder than all the other animals of the forest.

Back in Yaoundé, I had lunch with someone at the university, who asked me if I'd visited Céline. I went to Valérianne and Toussainte's, I said, but not Céline's, no. He laughed: Céline, the writer. In *Journey to the End of the Night*, the place Céline calls "Topo" is Campo. "We didn't go to Topo. There was no reason at all to go to Topo." Today, just like in that *Journey* to the end of the insomnia of that century, malaria and typhoid are rife in Campo.

The Ntem River, nicknamed the "Little Congo," as in Céline's novel, remains unchanged.

Louis-Ferdinand Céline was overwhelmed by insomnia, as well as by the slavery he witnessed, his fever and delirium, and the nocturnal commotion of the frogs. "Stuff cotton in your ears," he advised, and if you don't have that "use the nap of a blanket and a drop of banana oil. You can make very nice little plugs that way." But it is also at the mouth of the Ntem River that Louis-Ferdinand meets goodness in the figure of Alcide, the only kind person in the novel—although nothing distinguishes Alcide from the other colonial crooks. "After a while I got up to look at his face. He was sleeping like everybody else. He looked quite ordinary."[25]

At the mouth of the Ntem River

VI

End Up Sleeping?

Sleep in peace when day is done
That's what I mean
—Nina Simone, 1965[1]

"When a man is asleep," wrote Proust in a famous sentence, "he has in a circle round him the chain of the hours, the sequence of the years, the order of the heavenly host."[2]

And I too used to sleep.

Nostalgia for Sleep

I remember my invincible nights, back when I slept.

The summer of 1991, the end of a tour of the United States by train—Seattle to Boston nonstop, three days of panoramic scenery, the Pacific Ocean, the forest, the Rockies, the Great Plains, the Great Lakes, the big cities, the Atlantic Ocean. After a while the seats get uncomfortable so I lie down on them. The ceiling is a framework of dusty springs. I fall asleep to the slow rhythm of the American train. A night on the tracks, dead straight all the way. My young bones rest easily on the boards, the train runs ahead automatically on hypnagogic rails ... What better night is there than when you're traveling? I wake up in a different place from the day before. Simply through the momentum of the journey, my eyes open to another city: nonstop sleep, arrival at Boston station.

The summer of 1993, hitchhiking in Jordan with the man I love, whose initials are O.R. (*or*, the word for "gold" in French), and who will become my first husband. O.R. was an insomniac. I could rely on him to stay awake and keep an eye on things. The longer he stayed awake, the better I slept. It was a long haul in various trucks all the way to Petra, where the unguarded tombs, in the pink and ochre seams of the ancient rock, were used by travelers as sleeping spots. Back in Amman, at the dollar-a-night Cliff Hotel, we sleep on the roof with other backpackers. The mats are full of fleas. It's a mild evening. I drift off to sleep. The nightclub below is blasting out techno music at high volume. I sleep deeply, as if the flow of my dreams is in harmony with the electronic rhythms.

O.R. wakes me up in the morning and takes this picture; he finds my sleep miraculous.

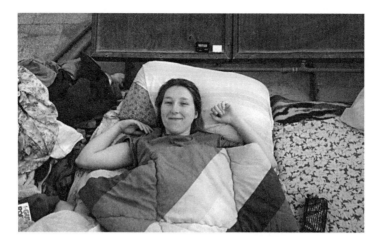

The summer of 1995, in North Cape, Norway. Midnight in the bright orange sky. Just arrived, filthy, in front of a beer that costs as much as a meal, we watch the sun not setting. It descends, touches the sea, gives a bit of a thrust, then rises toward another day. This sun that bounces back up as soon as it nudges the sea, red from the effort, makes me sleepy. We go outside into the polar wind and look for a hollow in the rocks. Somehow or other, we set up our tent. Not a single tree. The wind is horrendous. O.R., tall and athletic, sticks the tent pegs through the lichen while I slip into my sleeping bag. I fall asleep. With every gust the tent squashes flat onto my face, and I have visions of O.R. holding the tent poles firm in this wild, desolate place, O.R. battling the elements so that I have the space, the time, and the trust in him to sleep.

Hitchhiking in Norway,

and in Patagonia—schools of patience, very long territories with jagged coastlines

Christmas, 1996. *Pig Tales*, published at the end of August, has transformed my life. I am happy, very tired, and, among other surprises, I am rich, richer than anyone has ever been before in my family; except perhaps for my Basque great-great-uncle Agustin Olazabal, who emigrated to Buenos Aires, where he owned a whole block of apartment buildings. The mysterious plundering of our inheritance shocked our family of semi-Catholic, semicommunist fishermen, and impoverished them even further with the cost of the procedures undertaken in Argentina, where a cousin, Beltrand Aramburu, was sent as an emissary.

Certificate of indebtedness, May 19, 1899

Ninety-seven years after my ancestors' administrative disputes, I buy two plane tickets for Argentina—it's a dream of mine, an extravagance. I sleep so deeply during the thirteen-hour trip that the flight attendant wakes me to insist I drink some water. In Buenos Aires, I'm dead on my feet. Yes, when it comes to means of transport, the airplane is much faster than hitchhiking, but my brain can't keep up. O.R. locates the bus station; the only moment I'm awake is when he needs my Basque Spanish at the counter. I sleep in the bus for two days, opening my eyes in fits and starts when we stop at places with military names, General Rodriguez, General Conesa; or melancholy names, Azul, El Pensamiento; or the Basque names that are everywhere, Gorostiaga, Olascoaga, Uriburu, Ansoategui. I locate them on the map. Memories in the shape of dreams. A single file of travelers piling suitcases beneath a lamppost. La Pampa is flat, vast, even bigger than I had expected. Figments from daydreams dash around, herds of animals disappear among nameless plants. At the drop-off points, Basque shepherds welcome the "swallows" from the civil war.[3] All of a sudden we arrive in Trelew, the capital of Chubut. I remember drinking tea in a Welsh bistro called Dragon. O.R. rents a car. I fall asleep again.

When I wake up, in a Southern Hemisphere dawn, I have slept one hundred hours, four days. It's not sleep, it's renewal. O.R. has parked the car at the end of a track near an abandoned hut. He's not there, but I know he's not far away. I drink all the water I can find in the car and I walk in the sand; the air is pure, bracing. I'm totally awake, heading into the world's morning.

I reach the top of a cliff; there are sleeping sea lions as far as the eye can see.

Another life begins.

That was the period in my life when I slept. (Just like the sea lions I saw on a beach in Chubut.)

I took sleep for granted. I slept for twelve hours straight; it was my time. I was like the "sleeping woman" in *Time and the Room.* I kept sleeping no matter what happened in the room or over time.[4]

O.R. and I ended up separating.

I would continue sleeping in the same way until 2001, when a baby emerged from me.

Sleep Like a Baby

I was born with a malformed uterus. The cavity of a normal uterus opens out into a beautiful stretchy triangle. My uterus, shaped like a skinny *Y*, looks like an estuary with zigzagging branches. A laconic sonographer, ultrasound printouts in hand, once showed me: "On the left a normal uterus, on the right yours."

I'd made a drawing of it because I didn't have words to describe it.

The malformation had been caused by diethylstilbestrol (DES), an endocrine disruptor I had been exposed to as a fetus, inside my mother's womb. Diethylstilbestrol is a *teratogenic* drug: one that can cause birth defects, from the Greek *teratos*, "monster."[5] Due to lack of room in my deformed womb, my son was born very prematurely. He spent a month in an incubator, and on May 2 we took him home, minuscule but in good health.

From that moment on we became a family. And sleep began to get away from me. Our door opened to the baby and my sleep stole away like a cat. It saw the baby and said: It's him or me.

Note that while he was in the incubator—days of happiness, days of anguish—I slept. Even during the most difficult nights, the father of the baby and I slept. Then we would return to the incubator and talk to him.

We'd speak to him so that he'd come home with us.

And on May 2 , 2001, the baby knocked on the door, alive and well, and he said to me: From now on you will feed me at any hour of the day and night, you will bathe me and cuddle me and you will worry about me, and I will stop you from sleeping and writing, and you will be more bored than you have ever been before, feeding me my bottle, my fruit drinks, my solid food, playing with my giraffe, and you will be so exhausted that you will become fascinated by the idea of suicide, but *you would give your life for me*, and that sentence is not a cliché, it is the truth.

The baby arrived and he altered the meaning of sentences. He took them back to their basic, commonplace meaning.

But I didn't realize straightaway that my sleep had left me. At night a baby wakes up and wakes you. Especially a very premature baby. He had missed out on two months of warmth in my belly. His tiny stomach could take very little milk. The muscles in his mouth were too weak to suckle. His eyes were scarcely developed enough for the light. He knew nothing about the cycle of the sun. Didn't everything seem like a difficult night to him? A night that was constantly interrupted by urges, discomfort, pain, and big flashes of white that were, in between naps, daytime?

While I was breastfeeding, I watched *Loft Story*, the first reality TV show in France, based on the *Big Brother* format. It helped me get a grip on time. I remember watching Loana, the eventual winner, sleeping while I was floating in a sleepless night and in a bath of milk. From April 26 to July 5, 2001 (I found the dates on the internet), those people-characters, whose stories were taking place 24/7 without me having to make the slightest effort, distracted me from motherhood. That unedited, televised voyeurism resulted in a benign addiction, at a time when I was completely incapable of reading, scarcely capable of writing, and even less of sleeping.

I watched Loana get bored, a vacant face, the face of the human condition, icon of the 2000s, and my life without sleep began.

Then came the second baby, my first daughter, also born at seven months. Then came a third little life, who passed away before birth—a *miscarriage*, to use that unfortunate term—which was a real sadness. Then came the third baby, my second daughter, born dancing at eight months. And each new astonishing arrival chased away beneath her little feet whatever small amount of sleep I had left.

The babies "slept through the night," while my nights were full of broken sleep. As my children learned to sleep, I unlearned. It's hard to believe, but I had exchanged my sleep for that of my babies. And yet shouldn't I have slept, since they slept?

But how could I sleep, since they are mortal? Mortal like my brother, a baby forever.

No longer sleeping, one of us young parents ended up on the couch. Nocturnal choreographies of our thirty-something bodies folded and unfolded like sofa beds, waking and falling back to sleep badly, in unusual positions; the babies, still appearing suddenly between us, rolling on the rug, hurtling around on all fours, and us longing to escape, leaving them in the arms of others, for the duration of those nights stolen from time, and so the chaos increased until it took shape and became a family.

Famille de suricates (Meerkat family),
drawing by Nelly Blumenthal

Have a Nap?

"Sleep when he sleeps," they advised me when I was writing *The Baby*.[6]

The nap, what a nightmare. As soon as I lay down: an explosion of thoughts. The recommended "letting go" made me imagine falling off a cliff: a huge hand squeezing my head as I thrashed my legs in the air, my neck yielding, my body falling, and my head remaining there—on the pillow.

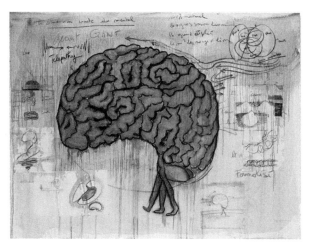

Fabrice Hyper, *Cerveau rapide* (Quick brain), 2010 (photo by Marc Domage)

How, while I was relaxing, could I have prevented my head from taking advantage of my letting-go in order to take up the entire space? All the words contained in my cranium transformed my whole being into a head. The body usually obstructs thoughts, the muscles fighting against the total invasion of the head, but my body, my ally, surrendered as soon as it was lying down.

Now that I had become a head, I had to get up, I had to walk, I had to find my legs again so I could restrain the surge of sentences. I would pile up mountains of words as if they could stand in the way of the death of my children, and I would wake up, *bang*, at four in the morning, with recurring nightmares of loss and disaster. And during the day my very lively children wore me out.

A Brief Stay with the Living and *White* were written in this way, from 2001 to 2003, at a boil.

No matter how much I told myself, like Raymond Queneau, "I can't sleep and I don't care, I organize my life differently," I couldn't see how to organize my life differently.[7] No matter how much I told myself, like Jacques Rigaut, "Sleep, insomnia … nothing there to make a fuss about," I could already write a whole book about it.[8]

The evening, around six o'clock. Six o'clock, faced with the children when I haven't slept. The tunnel from six o'clock to eight o'clock, when fathers are who knows where, doing something more *important*—not all fathers, but at any rate the father of my children, with all his attributes, attributes not lacking in Raymond Queneau, who around six o'clock would have been at Café de Flore having drinks, or else still in his office at Gallimard working on the future of literature, but perhaps not bathing babies.

I like Jean-Yves Jouannais's essay *Artists without Works*, about those writers, all men, who *preferred not* to write.[9] But so many countless female writers have remained without works, and it wasn't through some Dadaist disdain or dandyish desire. It was because they sometimes had thirteen children on their hands. See Virginia Woolf's *A Room of One's Own* et cetera.

Bathtime is a blessed moment, bathing three adorable children, except when I'm exhausted. Or when I want to write.

Hitting a wall at the end of the day. You'd like to lie on the couch with the newspaper. You'd like to hang out at the cinema. You'd like to perk yourself up at a bar. You could even stretch to a yoga class. No, you couldn't.

You have to grit your teeth and undress one or all of the recalcitrant children, who are also tired, a tired child is a tiresome child, take off nappies, wipe bums, run the water at the right temperature, not too hot, not too cold, stick your elbow or the thermometer in, follow the safety and hygiene recommendations, supervise the children, entertain them, console them, motivate them, prepare the meal at the same time or reheat who knows what, the fridge is empty, your spirits are low, but there are so many people more miserable than you in the world so you pour yourself a big glass of red wine.

That's what it was like during my children's childhoods. I was half-drunk as I proceeded with the routine and with the overflow of love in the tunnel from six o'clock to eight o'clock.

I headed off on trips. I left all that behind me. My books saved me: the translated editions of them justified my escapes. When I got home, the children were alive, clean, and fed, and happy to see me again. Yes, they had a father. Who was happy to see me again too. And they had grandparents.

Then the children grew up. They no longer required the total availability that little *Homo sapiens sapiens* are raised to expect of their mothers.

Because now, at six o'clock, no one needs me. Or it can wait. What a joy. What a soothing thought. *No one needs me.* I lie down (it could also be two o'clock in the afternoon, that diabolical time of day when the sun at its zenith does not cast a single shadow), I lie down and my fatigue morphs into a gentle wave. Dream water washes over the scalding sensation around my eyes. As if I had peeled away my ever-vigilant reflection. It retreats back where the ghosts are sleeping.

I have learnt to take a nap.

When I wake up—sometimes only a few minutes is enough—I don't feel like drinking alcohol, instead I feel like a big glass of carbonated water or a short walk outside. Traces of my dreams are still with me. It's a light sleep I wake from, and yet I'm returning from another world. The evening gets started. It is once again possible to live.

Critical Moments in Chronic Insomnia

But I'm not saying it was the babies who plunged me into insomnia. That insomnia, which became chronic, was accompanied by attacks of extreme insomnia—not a single deep sleep—including one long period of my life when someone I love was in a very bad way. Does one have the right to sleep when the other person is at death's door? Does one have the right to stop being attentive? Does one have the right to seek rest? And why the night rather than the day, when the night is so dangerous for those who are the most vulnerable? These questions, which I asked myself a thousand times, were accompanied by a totally insomniac mode of thinking: at the very moment I was falling asleep, I started to recount, in my head, the drama of our situation in life. It was not a particular situation itself but the account of it that stopped me from sleeping, the account being like the outcome or the sequel of the situation. Instead of sleeping I was recounting and recounting, mentally laying out life in words, looking for the best summary possible (very long), the best account (multiple). It was no longer life that was stopping me from sleeping but the twists and turns of its telling. I would formulate sentences, their sequencing, their rhythm. I was writing, without writing. My imaginary interlocuters changed, I exhausted them one after the other—my therapist, my best friend, a relative, even a passing acquaintance—because all my distressed brain was looking for was a way to endlessly adapt the most accurate story to the best listener.

Repairing Sleep

It couldn't go on any longer—insomnia's mice, the holes in the net of my nights. The Castrol oil drum going *glong glong* in my head.

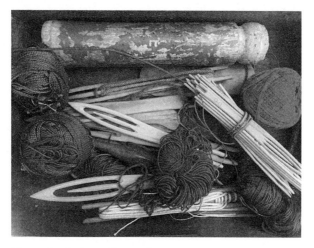

My grandmother's mending supplies

In the absence of a sleeping machine or a virtuoso *ramendeuse* such as my grandmother to repair my net, I decided to make an appointment at the sleep center at the Hôtel Dieu Hospital in Paris. There was a two-year waiting list. I ended up consulting a psychiatrist specializing in insomnia—

a "somnologist," as she described herself—who was president of an organization I had often consulted online: the Morpheus Network.[10] I liked the name. All those insomniacs gathered in a forum seemed to populate an underground world that ruled over the city during the night, like Fantômas used to.[11]

The first two months were simple: all I had to do was tick boxes in a "sleep diary," recording the hours when I slept and those when I didn't.

"Don't change anything," the somnologist told me. "Continue with your routine, including the alcohol and cigarettes." (Clearly I wasn't her first crazy person.)

By the end of the two months, my nights were no better than my days but I could *see* them. I could see the chart of my nights, especially the empty boxes designating no sleep.

She prescribed a *polysomnographic examination*. A sleep technician turned up one night at my home. He spoke to me about his dog as he stuck electrodes all over me, and I introduced him to Odette, my dog, still very young, who looked at us and laughed. In fact the whole family laughed as they watched the operation. I had sensors on my forehead, chin, torso, belly, and arms, and on my ankles if I remember correctly. They were itchy. It was seven o'clock in the evening. I couldn't sit still. "Do not go out like that," warned the technician. "The cops will arrest you." We negotiated that he would come back at nine the next morning: as he couldn't make it any earlier, as he had to walk his dog and I was not the only insomniac he had to unplug.

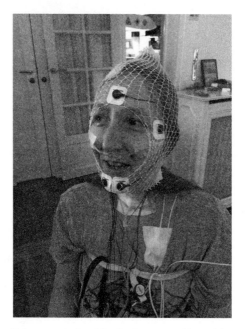

Polysomnography of the Darrieussecq subject, night

As the somnologist had told me not to modify anything in my lifestyle, I was expecting to sleep after two or three glasses of Haut-Médoc and some Stilnox. I had thought about Lexomil, but the effect is too mild: I wanted to be knocked out. In my harness, I needed one and a half pills to get six hours of passable sleep, which would be enough to *study my disorder.*

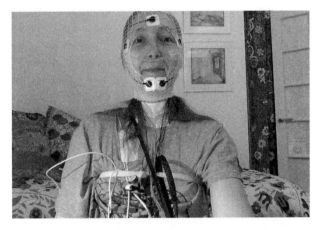

Polysomnography of the Darrieussecq subject, morning

In the morning, the technician removed the electrodes while we chatted. He lived near a forest and always found a few moments around the middle of the day to walk his dog. We both agreed: three walks a day for a dog. One of the reasons that I met Odette was because the somnologist had prescribed a lot of walking. Already in 1920, it was recommended by the doctor in Zamyatin's novel *We*: "As to the insomnia and for the dreams you complain of, I advise you to walk a great deal."[12] Walking promotes sleep, and a dog promotes walking. Odette takes me for walks.

A week later, I received the interpretation of the curves on my sleep graph: no sleep apnea, no oxygen desaturation; but

I was waking up twenty times an hour. It's normal to wake up two or three times an hour: a good sleep smooths the crests in the curve that the sleeper isn't aware of. But *twenty* times—these microawakenings were keeping me awake.

"Hypervigilance" was the verdict.

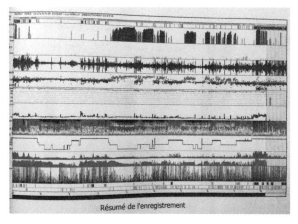

Résumé de l'enregistrement

I'm the pilot. You can't make me sleep.

So, objectively, I was suffering from a sleep disorder. *Hypervigilance*: in other words, a wakefulness disorder. And what is a wakefulness disorder if not a life disorder? Having a name for my disorder, I was already sleeping a bit better. I continued with my Bordeaux-based regime, but I undertook to reduce my intake of sleeping pills. And the high priestess—my name for the somnologist—prescribed a radical lifestyle change, which had nothing to do with the punitive methods of Huysmans. The idea was to *compress sleep*, to spend as little time as possible in bed. A bed is made for sleep. Potentially for a sex life. But it's no place to spend one's life.

No reading in bed, no eating, and no working in bed. La Bruyère already attributed this sensible instruction to Asclepius, god of medicine, in his temple in Epidaurus: Irene "cannot sleep at night, and he prescribes her not to lie a-bed by day."[13]

"Get up," ordered the high priestess, "and reserve your bed exclusively for use at night."

> *Forgive me, dear reader. I once used to write in my Roman garden, lying on my favorite couch.*[14]

In the past I would write in my king-size bed on memory-foam pillows. My children came and played PlayStation and we ate biscuits. I listened to music there, the children jumped and danced around. The sheets were full of crumbs, ribbons, bits and pieces. It was a party in the bed. I lived my life in my bed.

> *Now, as the light vanishes, I am tossed around on the whim of the waves.*[15]

Literature is all about lost paradises and insomnia.

The error of insomniacs is not so much to believe that we can never get our sleep back again—let's not get carried away—but that we can catch up on lost sleep. You can hardly ever catch up on lost sleep. Lost sleep, like paradise, is a golden age, it's nostalgia.

The high priestess told me to give up any hope of sleeping in. She said I had to set my alarm for the same time every day. Very early. Including weekends and holidays. Even if I haven't slept. "And," continued the high priestess, "you have to go to bed every evening at the same time. So you don't miss your train." The sleep train. The one that arrives approximately every two hours, *choo choo* to signal its cycle.

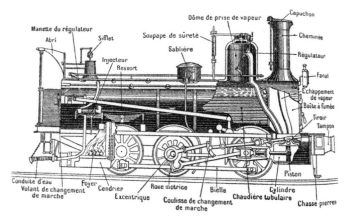

"Party's over. No more reading. Every night at midnight, and not before, get to bed! Wake up no later than seven o'clock. *And that's already a lot of sleep.*"

Thanks to this drastic scheduling of my time and space, I fall asleep. Deeply. It works. At midnight I rest my head on the pillow. At five past midnight the train arrives, and, after a brief trip through the hypnagogic mountains, I am no longer there. It's extraordinary. I often want to go to bed earlier, but no, midnight is when my locomotive turns into a pumpkin.

Alas, I continue to wake up at 4:04 a.m. In short, after two train cycles, I need at least one more for a restful night.

Uncompromising, the high priestess advised me to start my day the minute I wake up. "So it's four in the morning and the city is asleep? Shower, coffee, toast, and get to work."

I followed this rhythm when I wrote *Our Life in the Forest*: 4:04 a.m., get up; 4:44, get to work. At 7:00, the rest of the family got up, I took a break, served cereal to the children, helped the youngest to get dressed. Their father took them to school. At 8:08, the house was empty. I would keep writing until around midday. When I say "writing" … whatever time it is, every sentence is paid for with its pound of flesh. With its kilos of boredom and nothingness, of sordid loneliness, of fear of the grey screen. Eight hours of stagnation for eight sentences.

In the middle ages, explained the high priestess, people went to bed at sunset. That was the *first sleep*. They would wake up a few hours later, light the fire again, eat, make love, chat. Then go to bed again for the *second sleep*. That was the normal rhythm. Normal and medieval.[16] Described today as *biphasic sleep*, it's also, I read later, a common sign of old age.

But I didn't really want to live like they did in the middle ages. I was forty-seven years old. I wanted to *stay asleep*. Sleep through, like writing in one go (except writing like that hardly ever happens).

Around midday, I tried to have a nap. Most of the time I didn't succeed, and my eyes started to melt beneath my eyelids. Each eye, a volcano, was digging a crater in my skull. My eyeballs pulled on the optic nerves and subsided like lava in the soft, grey, living cavity of that which thinks and does not sleep. My first psychoanalyst, the one who saved my life, explained to me how the first lobotomies were very simple: all they needed was a little ice pick—he even said a *pencil*—to pierce through the orbit, *crack*, and sever the cause of our mental disturbances. The inventor of the procedure received the Nobel Prize in 1949. The story goes—I don't know if it's true—that he mostly operated on women.

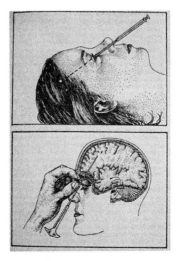

Transorbital lobotomy

Sometimes I succeeded with the nap. It was like a second sleep. With earplugs and all the shutters closed. I set the alarm for when school got out. My clandestine nights, my stolen nights, my daytime nights … I no longer had a social life, I didn't go out to lunch with anyone, I no longer did any sport, I ate whatever, whenever. In this rhythm, it was very difficult for me to fall asleep at a time that fitted in with other people's lives. I ended up writing all night, and sleeping when I could. I missed daylight.

Perhaps, when I no longer have any childrearing obligations, *when no one needs me anymore*, I'll adopt this quietly antisocial rhythm. But *when no one needs me anymore* is a version of death.

I always wake around 4:04 a.m. That part of the night remains an impasse.

Wanting to Sleep

I want to sleep. It's what I want. I can't do it. I don't know how to sleep. I am failing at good health practices. My "sleep debt" is accumulating.[17] I owe sleep to someone. To whom? To everyone who can't sleep for *real* reasons? To my brother who died so young? To the children who will live on this planet we've laid to waste? To the dead? To shadows? To whom? To what?

And yet: I want to sleep. It's what I want.

But everyone knows: In order to dance, it's not enough to *want* to dance. In order to write, it's not enough to *want* to write. One doesn't want to write, one writes. To a certain extent, the book writes itself, *despite* the wish to write—it writes itself in the very act of writing. Like a burst dam. "When I dance, I dance," said Montaigne.[18]

The same goes for sleeping: in order to sleep, you can't want to sleep. There must be *somniacs* who consider their sleep like a muscle they need to exercise. "Sleep decides for itself": this was said to me by one of those athletes who sleep to order, five hours a night, an efficient, concentrated, deep sleep; dead to the world, my ideal sleep. But the insomniac comes up against the paradox of the *decision to sleep*. How can you want the thing that should be taken for granted? It's impossible to *decide* to dance gracefully ... Wanting spontaneity means tensing up. Wanting to forget means remembering again. And wanting to fall in love means a marriage of convenience.[19] "To wish consciously to sleep," said Doctor Zhivago, with good reason, "guarantees insomnia."[20] Insomnia feeds on the effort to sleep the way ghosts slake their thirst on our fear.

So what to do? *Let go*, if only we hadn't been worn out by that instruction in the media 24/7.

Wait? But wait for what?

To create the right disposition for sleep? *Disposition* is the word used in hypnosis and in Daoism. And also in psychoanalysis. The famous "evenly suspended attention": listening to a patient is like contemplating a fire, drifting among the shapes of the flames, and then an ember erupts, or the fire dies. You pick up the ember (with tongs), gently kindle the flame, or sometimes add a log: it's an attentive dream state. It is not-waiting.

Do not wait for sleep?

In his book on hypnosis, François Roustang cites the Zen example of the apprentice archer. The apprentice archer takes aim, trying his utmost, changes the position of his hand, tightens his grip this way and that way … and hits the target. But the master dismisses this apparent success. Because it's not about "tricks to mime spontaneity." It's about not aiming for anything. Aiming is just another way of wanting. "Something has just been released," says the master, finally approving. It's like hearing the "it writes itself" of the nouveau roman.[21]

"It sleeps" is the state in which I dream. Something is sleeping.

Being neither an archer nor particularly Zen, I am going to use the very modest example of the cup-and-ball game. As a child, I didn't know how to *succeed* at this game. I aimed. I threw the ball in the air, followed the trajectory of the piece of string, tried to insert the spike into the orifice—incidentally, that's how I figured out, by deduction, the Big Secret about Sex. But nothing worked: not speed, not dexterity, not cunning. I kept missing. One day I understood that I shouldn't have been aiming. I shouldn't even have been wanting to aim. It was about being there. Concentration without a subject, an unpremeditated gesture of the hand, mind empty, eyes unfocused, and a great silence in oneself. At the heart of this silence, the future becomes one with the little object. It's going to happen—

it happens. Do not visualize what must take place. No. But something breaks through. Time rolls into a ball at the end of the string. There is no aim, since the aim has been achieved. *Clack.*

Queen of the cup-and-ball game.

It can be transposed to badminton, tennis, to more noble games. To higher, more noble stakes.

It's easy.

So why does sleep put up so much resistance to the queen of the cup-and-ball game?

"Intense generalized wakefulness" is how Roustang describes hypnosis; it seems to me that insomnia is the painful flipside of this. While I'm stagnating at 4:04 a.m., unable either to sleep or to write, I am in a piteous state of intense generalized wakefulness. I'm in a waking dream. I dream very hard. My imagination devours me: "it knows no sleep" (Roustang).[22] My white-hot ego concentrates itself into a dot, so tiny it vaporizes … molten cast iron, a burnt hole through which "the zone" opens up … where other zones open up, infinitely recurring until the point of disorientation … or creation, sometimes … or sometimes, yes, until the point of sleep … Yes, the ego must cease to exist … pulverized into a halo over which the world travels, along with the traveler ... a black hole ... a supernova ... a consciousness drifting in the night, the center of which is everywhere and the circumference nowhere ...

How exhausting.

ADÃO

My friend Adão Iturrusgarai, Basque-Brasilian-Patagonian, sent me this *Portrait de l'autrice en insomniaque* (Portrait of the author as an insomniac).

The good little soldier ego, the pilot ego, the chatterbox ego, the communicating ego, the worried ego, the good-dog ego, the accountant ego, the conquering ego, the sun ego, the *Moonstruck Pierrot* ego, the brave ego, the unfortunate ego—all those egos must let "something" write and dance. And, perhaps, sleep.

The ego is not detestable. But it can get in the way. Like a piece of furniture. The absence of oneself that is necessary for writing, including autobiography, is not a question of morality; it's more a question of furniture arrangement. If writing means pushing away the ego in order to make room, is sleeping the same?

Where the ego was, that's where the book will be. Where the ego was, that's where sleep will come. The sleep ego.

It writes itself. A gentle trance. Every now and again. In *fits and starts*. Often, I cling to my ego too much when I write. That's why it's difficult. There's no need to be insomniac in order to write. But one must accept *not to* write in order for there to be a sentence.

All the anxiety was necessary. But, suddenly, it writes itself.

Exorcism: when I have put the final full stop at the end of this book, my eyelids will grow heavy. A spell. A potion. My insomnia will dissolve in this book. The book will save me. When I hold the printed version in my hands, I will fall asleep.

Interlude

Plane on the runway, Kinshasa, November 2014

The plane is there, I saw it from the taxi, it's often the only plane on the runway, Air France, so white, so beautiful, the red, white, and blue tail like a rooster, and we always take off at night, but there are still a thousand checks to be carried out and other hassles, especially in Kinshasa, it's a long story, it's forty-five degrees in Niamey, thirty-five degrees in Haiti, thirty-eight degrees in Douala, thirty-three degrees in Kinshasa, but I have my French passport and I have money and the plane is there, on the other side of the window pane, I'm engaged in endless discussions, according to my information all my papers are in order, but according to local requirements there's one document missing, or two, or three, the total varies, and the world is very complicated, and unequal, and chillingly simplistic, at some point, whatever happens, I am going to fly off and they are going to stay. Anxious, bustling children are clinging to me, still wanting to help with my handbag, in the afternoon I dropped off my luggage in a backroom office in the center of Kinshasa, it's mandatory but I don't know if my luggage followed me here, the crowd is alarming, the rain is adding to the racket, I have to stop the street-porter thugs from hitting the children, I have to stop them from *protecting* me, I feel dizzy with how exhausting, rushed, and also comic everything here is, because the Kinshasans flying out to Panama are making fun of the whole situation, and of me in particular, everything is sticky, we're dripping with sweat, the plane is there, night is falling, all of a sudden I stop talking and getting agitated because something shifts and I'm moving forward and somehow I get through the half-open glass door along with a fireman who looks a bit crumpled and disoriented, I cross the damp tarmac restraining myself from running and I climb the metal walkway, *clong clong clong*

and then

an Air France stewardess gives me a glass of champagne

the air is cold and dry and that ambient spacey music is playing

I wipe my face with perfumed wet wipes

I look out at the airport through the plane window and request a second glass of champagne and I already feel infinitely safer

and I am infinitely grateful for the existence of France with its beautiful red, white, and blue planes and for a moment I confuse France with my mother

(usually once I land I remember that I am Basque)

and as usual in planes after all the difficulties very often yes right after takeoff I enter into the hypna-gogic state

dreams pass by the plane window

I fall asleep staring out at the scattered lights of magni-ficent, ruined Kinshasa, the exhausting city full of promise, yes I fall asleep as soon as I'm in the sky

I fall asleep off the ground

I fall asleep in the artificial gravity of aircraft cabins

I fall asleep perched up high in the atmosphere

I fall asleep as I leave the planet

I fall asleep beyond the sound barrier

that's what I need in order to fall asleep

nothing more is up to me

the pilot will deal with everything

VII

Insomnia Nights

Night's breath is your sheet, darkness lies down beside you. It touches your ankle and temple, it wakes you to life and to sleep.

—Paul Celan[1]

In 2014, on the minibus during my first trip to Rwanda, the country of the thousand hills, of the thousand ravines, where I was invited by an association for the prevention of genocides, we listened to slam poetry by the young Gaël Faye:

A sheet of paper and a pen, calm for a delirious insomniac
Exiled from Africa, far from my small country in the Great Lakes …
And here we are lost in the streets of Saint Denis
Before we get senile we'll go and live in Gisenyi …
Man I can't sleep anymore and I stay up like a zamu

A *zamu*, in the Great Lakes of Africa, is the guard in front of houses. Only those who have things to be stolen have *zamus*. One Sunday morning in Gisenyi I was chatting on the beach with a couple who were getting some fresh air. Lake Kivu stretched out before us like a Japanese landscape. They were Congolese. The wealthy inhabitants of Goma often came to this pretty beach resort on the Rwandan side of the lake "to spend a weekend where they felt safe."

The water was still and reflected the contour line of the volcanoes. A few pumice stones floated on the surface, islands quivered in the distance. The couple told me how much they dreaded returning on Sunday evening. During the weekends at Gisenyi, they slept deeply. The rest of the week they were in a state of constant vigilance. They had their routines in the little hotel on the edge of the beach, twenty minutes by taxi from their house in Goma—if they got through the border crossing okay.

A weekend where they felt safe … Thousands of years of volcanic activity have caused vast amounts of methane gas to accumulate in the depths of Lake Kivu. They say that one day the people living on the edges will be asphyxiated by a "limnic eruption"—a severe case of vulcanism. I have never slept very well on the shores of Lake Kivu, despite the beauty of the place. You have to trust the sleeping water in order to sleep feeling safe.

I was in Rwanda that time to listen to genocide-survivor testimonies, and in some cases to transcribe them in the

form of interviews. During another trip, in 2016, I led a writing workshop for survivors and former child soldiers from the whole Great Lakes area. I had a translator, whose name was Médiatrice. Médiatrice Uwingabire. She was eight during the genocide. She told me she had never been hungry "because she sucked her thumb." She would run through forests. One of the massacres happened in Ntarama, in the hills above the swamps of Nyamata. Since then she can no longer go near a forest. And she can't stand seeing piles of clothes, because she thinks "there's a body underneath." And yet Médiatrice told me that she slept well. Like a sinister lottery, some survivors sleep and others don't.

But when my Tutsi friends tried to explain to me what it meant to be seen as an insect, to be treated like a cockroach, an *inyenzi*, I thought of Gregor Samsa waking from his dream, transformed into a cockroach, lying there "the long nights through without sleeping."[2] The word *Gregor* comes from the Greek word for "awake," and means "to be vigilant, a watchman."

The Bisesero Genocide Memorial

During the testimonies, the issue of sleep didn't arise immediately, and sometimes it wasn't mentioned at all. How one sleeps is a very intimate subject. It evokes the bed, family, peace. And the couple, sex. It evokes a whole range of things, sometimes lost forever. I had to wait for chance moments, in the evening, over a beer, with those who, perhaps, dreaded going to bed. Thierry Sebaganwa spoke to me of his "fixation with always shutting the door to sleep. Impossible to sleep with a door that doesn't lock." Beatrice Uwera told me, on the contrary, of her fear of being locked in; she always had to have the door open. "My aunt never sleeps," said Consolatrice Mishirarungu. "She wanders around all night long with a flashlight. She looks in corners, under beds, et cetera. She can't handle it at all when her children go out to nightclubs. She calls them the whole time." And several others, who survived their children, confided in me about the urinary incontinence they had been plagued with for a long time, and how they stopped themselves from sleeping for fear they would wet the bed.

"Before, the word *trauma* didn't exist in the Kinyarwanda language. It had to be invented," said Assumpta Mugiraneza. I admired the therapies they came up with to help the survivors, the shelters, such as the Association of Widows of Genocide, for example. The women gathered there to weave bracelets, to earn a little bit of money; but the most important thing was to be together, not isolated, and to think about other things, to concentrate on the handiwork. It was a communal battle against, literally, the act of staying in bed. The radiant Sabine Uwase, director of the shelter, requested that the widows make their beds in the morning. It was a simple statement from her: "A woman who makes her bed won't go back to bed."

Insomnia is a well-recognized symptom in the clinics that treat major psychological trauma. Paul Alerini (a psychiatrist in Marseille) and Marie-Caroline Saglio-Yatzimirsky (a consultant at the psychotraumatology center for asylum seekers at Avicenne Hospital in Bobigny) spoke to me about their patients, refugees and displaced people, whose sleep is simply another form of exile. Their sleep is not restful, it is not a refuge. Even when they're asleep, the persecutor is there, that "woman in black" who hunts down Safia, who was threatened with female genital mutilation in her country: "I can't sleep because of her. I don't know who she is … I don't know who is coming after me. She frightens me … She wants to grab hold of me. She's panting. She wears me out at night."[3]

Insomnuit (Insomnight), painting by Lydie Arickx

Paul Alerini wrote to me on September 8, 2019, about L, a man who was beaten and tortured in Libya: "L still very frail, he has terrible nightmares in which his friends die before his eyes, he dreams that his daughter is taken away from him. He dug in his heels, then agreed to come … I gave him a packet of Xanax I had in a drawer. He took one tablet and slept for twelve hours straight." The effect of tranquilizers on someone who has never taken any. But sleep is not exchangeable. It can't be bought. You can't lend a bit of sleep to someone who has none.

"Everything comes back": in trauma clinics, it's what is called "intrusion."[4] Avoidance strategies then become an impediment to life, night and day. For years after the War of Independence, my father-in-law was woken by his nightmares from Algeria. In Hemingway's short story "Now I Lay Me," the narrator, who suffered a shrapnel injury during World War One, describes how, for many years, he stayed awake every night in order to stop his soul going out of his body: "I could only stop it by a very great effort."[5]

Kurt Vonnegut's *Slaughterhouse-Five* is a groundbreaking novel about what we now call "posttraumatic stress." It is also a case of *bearing witness through science fiction*—for Vonnegut, this genre alone is able to account for a dislocated reality. Billy Pilgrim is a former prisoner of war who has, like the author, survived the bombing of Dresden. He can't sleep. Despite having a big double bed and a gentle vibrator, "Magic Fingers," bolted to the springs of the mattress, he remains in the grip of insomnia. Admittedly, his wife snores (we learn in passing that she no longer has her ovaries or uterus, which apparently *helps her to sleep*—I should consider that). But if Billy, an optometrist from Ilium, New York, can't get a wink of sleep, it's because in exactly one hour he will be kidnapped by a flying saucer from Tralfamadore. The appointment was made beyond the dimensions of time and space, and Billy keeps being transported to the extraterrestrial zoo where he will be on display as a human specimen, then returned to Dresden in 1945, to the slaughterhouse that serves as barracks for the prisoners. A group of insomniacs, who hear his cry for help during his nighttime radio program, try to help him return home to Ilium in 1969, but forever more, until his death, Billy will continue to be sent back to the alien planet and to the bombs in Dresden.

The Europa Ferris wheel, set up in front of the slaughterhouse where Vonnegut was a war prisoner, Dresden, October 2016. The slaughterhouse, which was far from the city center, escaped the destruction of Dresden on February 13, 1945.

Billy Pilgrim no longer lives anywhere. Wherever he is, he is not there. There is no ground beneath him, the earth under his feet has disappeared, he will forever be a pilgrim, between our planet and elsewhere.

The slaughterhouse of our times is this *world without sleep* described, from the beginning of World War One, by Stefan Zweig. It has broken the human spirit, "scaring off sleep, chasing forgetfulness from every bed."[6] And Kafka, in his postwar diary, wrote on October 15, 1920: "I am not so forgetful as I used to be in this respect, I am a memory come alive, hence my insomnia."[7]

Surrealism, born from the war, is tied to insomnia. "The worst material conditions are fine," wrote André Breton in his *Manifesto of Surrealism*. "The woods are white or black, one will never sleep."[8] And Luis Buñuel slices open an eye with a razor in *Un Chien Andalou*, the first surrealist film, cobbled together with Salvador Dalí in 1929:

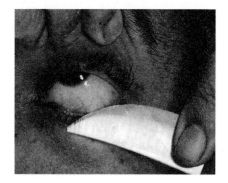

A single large, translucent tear leaks out, in which glimmers the century's insomnia.

For years I read and reread Georges Perec's *A Void*.[9] Fascinated by this metaphysical detective novel written without the letter *e*, dazzled by the author's inventiveness in getting round the absence of the most frequently used letter in French, I suggested to adolescents, in various writing workshops, in various cities, in various languages, that they take their chances with the book. I discussed individual solutions with Perec's translators—without *a*, without *o*, without *i*. But I hadn't understood that the book was about insomnia.

And yet it's the first line of the book: "Incurably insomniac, Anton Vowl turns on a light." It's clear for all to see, as clear as no *e*'s.

What the characters of the novel are missing has been so well erased that the missing thing itself leaves no trace. The dead disappear. The police investigators disband. The mourning cannot be accounted for in writing. And sleep no longer occurs. After trying everything—barbiturates, meditation, sport, nocturnal walking, and even removal of his sinuses—Anton Vowl commits suicide: "I did so want to sink into an alcoholic coma. I did so want to finish my days in a softly intoxicating and long dying torpor. But, alas, I cannot avoid … a void! Who? What? That's for you to find out! 'It' is a void."

Georges Perec, whose family was assassinated by the Nazis, wrote *A Void* devoid of them. Lost sleep is the sign of what has been voided. Vowl's insomnia is the hole left by the deaths during the Shoah. Sleep has been damaged. No one will ever sleep in the same way again. After such harm to human relationships, how could we sleep?

"What happened" is how Paul Celan names the destruction of the European Jews. I remember that sleep is one of the big issues in Elie Wiesel's *Night*, and that in the death march "to sleep meant to die."[10] I remember that Primo Levi, in the chapter "Our Nights" of *If This Is a Man*, writes about waking up in the camp as a nightmare within a nightmare, but also describes, in a famous passage, "man's capacity to dig himself in, to secrete a shell, to build around himself a tenuous barrier of defence, even in apparently desperate circumstances."[11] I remember that it was in terms of class struggle that Robert Antelme evoked sleep in the camps: "If they still want material to be SS with tomorrow, we've got to sleep.... Sleep is not a respite, it doesn't mean we've knocked off one day we owe the SS; it just means that we're preparing ourselves, through a task called sleep, to be more perfect prisoners."[12] I am standing in front of my library and every book opens on a unique voice, and on a unique night.

Charlotte Delbo stayed in bed for months after Auschwitz: "I kept a vague image of that time, one in which there isn't a light speck allowing me to distinguish between wakefulness or sleep."[13] Aharon Appelfeld, in *The Man Who Never Stopped Sleeping*, sleeps incessantly after the war: "In my sleep, I was connected to my parents, to the house in which I had grown up, I continued to live near them, we were never separated." Then he evokes the suicide of his companion Marc, another survivor, who had completely lost the ability to sleep.[14]

The books in my library, standing next to each other, vertical pages lined up, accommodate so many dead people, each one unique, all the dead, unique even down to their sleep, as if the needs of the human species—eating, drinking, sleeping—remained irreducibly in the *style* of each man, of each woman, down to the starkest privation.

An immense insomnia over the Earth. And in each of those individual shells is a person with breath of their own.

VIII

Other Bodies

Young plants grow at night.
So do children and young animals.
—Andrei Tarkovsky[1]

After the writing workshop with the genocide survivors in 2017, I traveled with my publisher to the Virunga Mountains, the meeting point, along the ridges of the volcanoes, of the imaginary boundary lines between three countries—Rwanda, the Democratic Republic of the Congo, and Uganda.

I wanted to have a break (perhaps sleep?) and see the gorillas. Our hotel in Ruhengeri had hosted the primatologist Dian Fossey, murdered in 1985 in the sanctuary she had created for the gorillas. The area was safer now than back then, but boundaries dissolve in the forest.

After four hours of climbing with guards and guides, we came upon a nest. Twenty or so gorillas were dozing as they munched on bamboo, all snuggled against each other. The guides had advised us to remain calm and silent as we crouched at the edge of the nest. The babies were monkeying around us, skipping and cavorting, and the adults nonchalantly extended a long arm in order to, *gotcha*, bring them back. Nothing happened, apart from this amazing connection between us. One species was looking at the other— we, especially, were doing the looking. The old male, a

The silverback, the patriarch with the silver back

silverback, glanced occasionally at our crouching species: we were piled on top of each other too, astonished, less hairy, and less used to being together than they were—they who owed their survival to this extreme tourism.

At that point there were eight hundred mountain gorillas in existence. A gorilla's hand is a trophy; they are made into ashtrays.

Sixteen hundred ashtrays.

But it's not only the gorillas that matter, it's all of us, it's our future as human and nonhuman animals on a single planet. And you have to really love the Sistine Chapel and the Great Pyramid of Cheops and the music of John Coltrane and the paintings of Shitao and all of literature in order to keep loving the human race.

Primo Levi granted more importance to human life than to that "of a crow or a cricket," but he was against suffering for all creatures. In *Other People's Trades*, he relates how, by error, he walked into a laboratory where scientists were conducting experiments using sleep deprivation: "The squirrel was exhausted: it trudged along that endless trail, and it reminded me of galley slaves, and those other forced laborers in China who were obliged to walk for days and days in similar treadwheels to pump water into irrigation canals. There was no one else in the laboratory; I switched off the motor, the treadmill came to a stop, and the squirrel fell asleep on the spot. Perhaps it is my fault that we still know so little about sleep and insomnia."[2]

Dear, wonderful Primo Levi.

Doesn't it mean we sleep a little less if we treat animals as objects? Or if we act as if there's us, and then others? Doesn't it stop us from sleeping, to act as if they didn't exist?[3]

"They Sleep and We Are Awake"

This was the naturalist Daubenton's definition of animals: "They sleep and we are awake." Because being awake is synonymous with reason. All through his article for Diderot's *Encyclopédie*, Daubenton takes on the role of a hunter, and the question, What is an animal?, restated over and over, runs ahead like a hare. Daubenton sends his colleague Buffon out as a torchbearer, and calls on Descartes, for whom man alone exercises reason, an animal being the equivalent of a machine. Man is, by definition, "he who does not sleep." Daubenton outlines a whole scale of plants and "animals like us," "full of beings more or less lethargic, more or less half-asleep." Because if man is awake, he can also be inert and like an automaton, "and I know of nothing more involuntary than a man buried deeply in thought, if it is not a man deeply asleep." So, his reasoning continues, what happens when a man sleeps or loses consciousness? Does he cease to be a man? Does he become an animal? Despite the classification of the *more or less half-asleep*, Daubenton seems troubled by the absence of any clear definition of beings who are alive yet asleep.

"Animals are spectators in the world," writes Jean-Christophe Bailly. "We are spectators in the world alongside them and simultaneously."[4] In this very moment, as I read and write, just before midnight, as the Eiffel Tower's beacon glides like the beam from a lighthouse over the roof, a pangolin is exploring its patch of forest, far away, in a bend of the Congo River. In this very moment. At the same time. He beholds the world. Within the bounds of this medium-sized planet, the pangolin arranges its own zone, discovers it, categorizes it, surveys it, digs around in it, crisscrosses it, sees it, smells it. I like to think that it reads it and writes it in its own way, then curls up in its nest and dreams.

Elsewhere, off an island in Thailand, a dugong watches the dawn, peering up through the water.

And in the courtyard of my building, close by, a pipis-trelle bat deciphers the zigzags of a moth with its radar.

The pangolin is the most poached animal in the world. It shares with the tiger and the rhinoceros the sorry privilege of being attributed, by the superstitious side of Chinese medicine, the power to stiffen droopy penises. In this case it's the pangolin's scales, but I'm not sure if they're supposed to be ground, implanted, or worn around the neck. In 2017, twelve tons of pangolin scales were seized from a Chinese freighter. I remember a pangolin nest in the forest in southern Cameroon. It was quite a wide area of soil that had been skillfully turned over, mixed with twigs. The pangolin only comes out at night; it is difficult to see, but not difficult to trap, alas. Back in the village the next day, there was a pangolin hanging up, hooked by its tail on the awning of a hut, for sale and ready to roast, because in this village no one cared less about the scales; they relished the meat, "like duck confit," someone told me later in Yaoundé. The pangolin must have been the inhabitant of the nest. I was so fascinated by the poor dead creature that the poacher thought I wanted to buy it. Completely uncoiled, like scaly duct tape, it was almost as tall as me. That bare belly, smooth and glistening, those enormous claws, that snout both trusting and betrayed … The creatures in *Star Wars* are not a patch on these imaginatively formed mammals.

Twelve tons of scales: How many pangolins?

Perhaps we stay awake, keeping watch, because we sense, despite everything, that we are not alone. Other beings have their eyes open. Other eyes are looking. Insomnia feeds off this bewildering feeling: there is something else.

Wild animals, dreams, and stars. These three things have something in common: they exist. Another thing in common: we forget them. Dreams exist in us. Stars exist above us. Wild animals exist alongside us. We forget them because our productivity would decrease if we took seriously the reality of dreams, the reality of wild animals, the reality of stars. And if we stopped repressing them (the dreams), eating them (the animals), forgetting them (the stars—that we are standing on a medium-sized planet in an immense universe spinning around without us). These three realms (the unconscious, life in the wild, and stars) exist in the same way: independent of our will.

It was by listening to the shamans of the Amazonian Napu Runa people that Eduardo Kohn, a forest thinker, understood that "dreams are not commentaries on the world; they take place in it."[5] The Napu Runa also interpret the dreams of animals. By moving away from this continuity, by breaking these ties, we lose that part of sleep that is another awakening. And we probably hasten our end.

For a while it was thought that the coronavirus had reached humans by way of the pangolin. The pangolin's revenge. Unintentional and chilling. A pangolin had supposedly been placed in contact with a bat on the animal stands of a market in Wuhan. But this hypothesis has since been disproved. We still don't know which animal was the missing link—apart from us.

These encounters between species are a sign of the times, and as absurd "as the chance encounter of a sewing machine and an umbrella on an operating table"—in the words of Lautréamont, a renowned predictor of catastrophes.[6] The pandemic has brought wild animals along with it, even into our lockdowns. Transmission occurs from dead animal to dead animal in a sort of barbaric inventiveness. Our trafficking creates monsters. Our deforestation drives out the animals. The sleep of our reason will kill us.

We are the sleepers. The animals are awake. They are on the alert, watching out for hunters. To sleep like a wolf is to wake up constantly. In a famous short story, Cortázar describes an axolotl as an animal without eyelids. The narrator is obsessed to the point of insomnia by these unsleeping salamanders in their aquarium. "Perhaps their eyes could see in the dead of night, and for them the day continued indefinitely."[7] At the end, he becomes an axolotl, he has always been an axolotl, it is him on the other side of the aquarium.

The axolotl, illustration from approximately 1880

The books we read to our children are full of bears, tigers, and lions. Our children fall asleep thinking about animals. We raise them with and against animals, as if it were vital, from the moment they are born, to instruct them that we are different—different and superior. We attribute thought and speech to animals, but by saddling them with our humanity. We turn them into monsters or soft toys. But the experience children have with their cuddly toys is the exact contradiction of Daubenton's article in the *Encylopédie*: the eyes of glass or plastic are open at night. The animal stays awake, watching over our little ones while they sleep.

And we keep it from our children for as long as possible that their bedtime companions are "endangered species." The disappearance in the coming years of tigers and lions.

Abandoned stuffed animal, Chernobyl Exclusion Zone, June 2018

The massacre of elephants and bees, but also of bumble-bees and earthworms and of all those creatures not in our fairytales, not in our heraldry, and not in the direct line of sight of our rapaciousness. *Endangered species* is a spurious expression inherited from the 1970s and 1980s. We need to talk, as Derrida did in his final seminar, of "total war against animals." The difference is not so much between us and animals as between the "killable" and the "non-killable," as Donna J. Haraway pointed out.[8] And in order to make humans killable, all you have to do is animalize them. Human massacres are permitted by animal massacres.

The war is here, the war on animals, the war on "killables." We sleep on their corpses. This war has produced such a mass of deaths that there now are only four thousand tigers in the wild, and five thousand in zoos. Twenty thousand lions "in the wild," most in wildlife parks. Even in a territory as landlocked as Eswatini, ex-Swaziland, I don't know if the lions can be counted as "wild". In 2014, in Hlane ("wild" in Swazi) National Park, I saw—yes, for real—lions in a landscape of savannas, like in children's books. The lion king was asleep under a tree, its belly extremely round after eating an antelope; the lionesses were licking their chops, the lion cubs were playing. It was a vision out of Eden (apart from the antelopes). We drove over to the giraffes; then to the elephants; then to the three white rhinoceros, the pride and glory of the park. Then to the enclosure. Down there in the bottom of Africa, Hlane National Park was like a larger version of the Thoiry ZooSafari, fifty kilometers outside Paris.

Chickens are the most ubiquitous birds on the planet. Pigs are as loveable as dogs. Octopuses know how to use tools. Fish feel pain.

After giving up eating mammals, then any animal I could not kill with my own hands (that is, all warm-blooded vertebrates, then all fish), I limited my input of animal proteins to "killable" shellfish and prawns. Then I learned that prawn fishing entails the simultaneous capture of, on average, twenty-six other species, whose corpses are thrown back in the sea.

Please leave me oysters. With a glass of Chablis.

What will we miss when the last orangutan is dead? A way of being? Gestures. A certain relationship with trees. Unique hands, which pick up things in a way our hands don't: a different type of contact. And those eyes contemplating the world.

What we will also miss is their invitation: to ask ourselves who they are; and so to ask ourselves who we are. This movement toward them extends us, creates space within us, creates dreaming. Their presence elevates us. Their disappearance diminishes us.

"There are some people who can live without wild things, and some who cannot." The opening line of *A Sand County*

Almanac, by an ecologist who was one of the pioneers of environmentalism.[9] Those who cannot live without wild animals lose sleep as the massacre continues. Their sleep unravels. It is populated with ghosts.

A pair of thylacines, or Tasmanian tigers, etching from 1883

The last caged Tasmanian tiger died in 1936. The last known Tasmanian tiger in the wild was killed in 1930. The only thing tigerlike about it was its stripes. It was a marsupial that looked like a dog, stocky, with a large jaw, its hindquarters somewhat low to the ground. Both the tiger and its cousin the "devil" bear the name of Tasmania, that magnificent island at the end of the world, also the site of a terrible genocide of Indigenous people. The stripes on the tiger foreshadow its death.

Old growth rainforest, Tasmania, 1999

Of the thylacine, its scientific name, all that remains are a few photos and a thirty-second film. The black-and-white images suggest a black-and-white animal, but it seems that it was brown and yellow. The images give it a slightly jerky gait, like in the Charlie Chaplin film *Modern Times*. The film is silent. Cry, howl, yelp? We will never hear its voice; its soundtrack in the world's concert is lost. The last of its species, the tiger in the Hobart Zoo paced around in circles like every caged animal. It used its paws to eat, like my dog. The Tasmanian tiger paced around for all slaughtered animals. It stands shivering in our memory for those others unknown to us, even in their absence.

Last known photo of a thylacine, Hobart Zoo, 1933

By amputating our lives from other lives, by removing their bodily gestures from the dance of the living, our world will soon be diminished. That feeling, both weighty and diffuse, is the "heavy heart" that Élisabeth de Fontenay talks about.[10] It's what Aldo Leopold speaks of: "For one species to mourn the death of another is a new thing under the sun."[11] It is sorrow: "I feel a great sorrow, an endless sense of mourning for every dead Animal. One period of grief is followed by another," says one of Olga Tokarczuk's narrators, an insomniac who tries to treat her sorrow with infusions of hops, along with valerian pills: "I am in constant mourning."[12]

It is not only the famous dodo—the lost dodo, so often ridiculed—that has disappeared through the actions of humans. Our alphabet of animals is also missing, since 2006, the baiji dolphin of the Yangtze River. Soon it will be missing the North Atlantic right whale; the babirusa from Indonesia, also called the "deer-pig"; the gharial, a species of crocodile that lives mainly in the Ganges; the Saharan cheetah; the Amur leopard from southeastern Russia; the Californian red wolf; the woolly spider monkey from southeastern Brazil; the okapi from the Ituri Rainforest in the Democratic Republic of Congo; the ploughshare tortoise from Madagascar; and still more living and unique creatures. And so the bestiary in our books is shrinking, the soundtrack of our nights is fading, and we are like the characters in *A Void*, tormented, no longer knowing what is no longer there.

Dodo skeleton, reconstituted from the bones of several specimens (National History Museum, London)

The mourning is phenomenal. Something inside us is dead "from not having met it."[13] And it is a mourning that for a long time was downplayed and mocked. Championing the cause of whales at the École normale supérieure in the early 1990s meant not being afraid of ridicule. Human relations prevailed, relations *between humans*: what we call "the economy," "culture," "politics," "justice," "equality," "liberty," "fraternity." We never managed to convince people that concern for what is human does not preclude concern for what is nonhuman; that, on the contrary, the programmed destruction of wild animals concerns us as a species. We were too few, too scattered and misunderstood. We lacked conceptual tools and left ourselves wide open to accusations of sentimentalism and anthropomorphism.

The major works by Isaac Bashevis Singer on vegetarianism were not yet translated into French, or were translated only in part, when he dared to say that, in relation to animals, "all people are Nazis; for the animals it is an eternal Treblinka."[14] Élisabeth de Fontenay's *The Silence of the Beasts*, published in 1998, introduced readers in France to an understanding of animals.[15] In our extremely Cartesian country, she was the first to dare to compare what at the time seemed incomparable: human suffering and animal suffering, the human slaughterhouse and the animal slaughterhouse. Human deaths, animal deaths: our destiny in common.

How do we sleep while our beds are burning? sang the Australian band Midnight Oil in 1987, a hit we all danced to back then.[16] The song denounces the theft of Aboriginal land, and the massive bushfires. But we didn't listen, we danced beneath orange skies.

The Third Eyelid

Baptiste Morizot, and others, pushed me out of my habitual ground—out of my *bed*.

As I write this book I watch my dog Odette sleeping. Such calm. Such abandon. Such economical use of energy. Such remarkable life skills: sleep as soon as nothing is required of you. Odette sleeps twelve or thirteen hours a day. If there were such a creature as a hybrid cat-dog, it would be her. She dreams. Her eyelids flutter. Her jowls tremble. Her paws shake. She is on the lookout at the edge of the zone, running in twilight, when a dog is indistinguishable from a wolf.

Sleep is a bridge between species. Our sleep is mammalian. We contemplate our sleeping companions.

Her eyes are half-open: her third eyelid, rimmed by a black line, makes her eyes look reptilian. On the internet I found out that it is the *nictitating membrane*, from the Latin *nictare*, "to blink." It is a translucent eyelid. It allows seals and sea cows to see in the water without damaging their corneas. Cats, some bears, rabbits, and hares also have one. Perhaps because they sleep a lot?

For Odette, a terrestrial but also quasi-aerial being, as swift as the wind, it is the membrane of dreams. Her sleeping eyes do not see outwardly but see within, into her own world; they see beyond, across, through. My humanity—Odette tells me—gives me access to only a partial world.

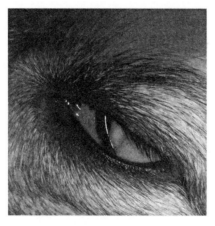

Odette asleep, her gaze veiled by the third eyelid

A third eyelid would be my salvation (I tell myself). My double eyelids are not enough. Under those closed eyelids the insomniac eye does not sleep: it sees blackness. It sees red if the light is bright, orange if the light is soft, it sees shadows and small blood vessels, it sees "fantastic fairylands," wrote Colette, a specialist in insomnia and animals.[17] Popular wisdom has it that when we are fatigued we can't see straight. Our eyes roll into another skull, gone to look elsewhere, inside someone who can sleep, under foreign eyelids like under foreign skies. So why not in another animal, in a dog, a cat, a hare? If my eyes were equipped with a third eyelid I would mutate. What sort of dream would I surrender to? What animal form would allow me to leave behind my insomniac identity, to slough off my sleepless skin?

"My child sleeps with his eyes open like a hare." *Mi niño duerme con los ojos abiertos como las liebres.* A traditional Andalusian lullaby …

Odette is a mixed-breed dog: a greyhound without a pedigree, a little shaggy whippet, a gazelle hound from Salies-de-Béarn, a slightly Afghan borzoi, but much lighter. Odette has the back legs of a hare, the haunches of a cheetah, the tail of a filly, the ears of a squirrel, the waist of a wasp, and a very long muzzle that is hers alone. I write in the company of this chimera.

Legendary for their loyalty, greyhounds sleep at the feet of recumbent statues. In the Basilica of Saint-Denis, or in the

Royal Monastery of Brou beside Margaret of Austria, these guardians at the entrance of the marble tombs wait forever for their dead masters to awaken.

Greyhound with eyes half-closed, Royal Monastery of Brou, Burgundy, by Nelly Blumenthal

4:04 a.m.

I turn on my computer. My file is there. *Pas dormir.* It glows and hurts my eyes. I no longer have any idea where I am at with it. I feel like a coffee, but if I drink a coffee, I will *never* get back to sleep. I heat water for an umpteenth herbal tea. Out the window the night does not look promising. I can't be bothered getting dressed, I'm in my madwoman's dressing gown, a uniform from a mental institution. I have to finish this book in order to be able to write the other books I have in my head and I keep changing the plan: I don't know if the "drowning" section, in my Conrad novel, has finally docked after the last section, or drifted into the preceding section, or tipped into the first section, and if this story on its tilted plane, this vertical floor, truly makes any sense in my insomnia.

"The author is by definition a person who is more than normally guided by an underlying uncertainty concerning the coherence of existence or whether there exists at all a word which enables us to talk with certainty about such things." Thus claims the insomniac writer in *Dark Branches*.[18] *More than normally*, I'm not so sure. Every speaking being is aware that words more or less adhere to the world. But writers are forever struggling with that, because their material is words. In insomnia, writes Mari Akasaka (the one who makes herself vomit in order to sleep), "I'd seen words falling to pieces."[19] There are a thousand reasons not to sleep, but that's just one of them.

I open up Kafka's diary again, the book I always have on my bedside table: "I believe this sleeplessness comes only because I write. For no matter how little and how badly I write, I am still made sensitive by these minor shocks, feel, especially towards evening and even more in the morning, the approaching, the imminent possibility of great moments which would tear me open, which could make me capable of anything, and in the general uproar that is within me and which I have no time to command, find no rest."[20]

I stand up and I stagger—it's not exactly from fatigue, or from alcohol, let's not exaggerate, I'm staggering from insomnia. I feel it in my legs, in my eye sockets, and in my shoulders. I feel the world toppling, the day encrusted in my nighttime eyes. And I know the ground is giving way under my feet and that insomniacs are maniacs in the desert of their boredom.

Pripyat, Chernobyl Exclusion Zone

How did we sleep, before, in the forests? How did we make do in the time of the forests? We were a group. A group in a cave. We kept warm in a nest, like gorillas. We had no doubt invented taking it in turns; even the guardsman has to let his guard down. Even the lookout has to close his eyes. In the caves, the adults kept watch over the children. There is very little record of prehistoric babies in the rock walls. It's rare to find the remains of their bones. So little they dissolved. But their hands are there. See the adults holding the babies in their arms to choose the placement of their hands among the larger handprints. See the adults carrying the future in their outstretched arms—that baby.

27,000 years ago, "negative hands" in the Caves of Gargas

Humanity kept growing, sunrise after sunrise, moon cycle after moon cycle. Then everything accelerated. Time overflowed space. Speed caught distance unawares. The urgency of the situation annihilated the horizon. Insomnia burned down the forest.

Nights when I would get lost in the forest. Nights when I would search in vain for the clearing. I am lost, and all the trees look the same. I am lost and the dawning of the book, which I saw yesterday, is abandoned in the wasteland of the night's thoughts.

Moon, the night of April 8, 2020

And then other nights ... All the possible books, the fragments of books, the bits of books, the bushes and thickets of books ... and the germination of a tree, the fertile tree, the one that will produce a book. The nights when the forest is a plentiful refuge—the nights when a peaceful plant kingdom's time merges with writing time, oh, for those auspicious nights ... The book wakes me up. A bud comes to life. A branch moves. The night of growth.

Poetry, like dreaming, speaks a wild truth. Sleep and insomnia, asymmetrical domains, open onto their own pathways. In the hypnagogic zone, we hear with our skin the way frogs do, with our lateral line like sharks, in our bellies like pregnant women. Vibrations guide us like they do spiders. We hear the trees. We move away from the straight line. We renounce our electrical stimulation, our frenetic consciousness, our branch-trimming common sense.

Henri Rousseau, *Le Rêve* (The dream), 1910 (Museum of Modern Art, New York)

"My burrow takes up too much of my thoughts," writes Kafka's confined creature. This text was left unfinished, like all Kafka's novels, as if what he was writing was too much for him. So we carry it. Reading the story, we carry Kafka on our back. "The Burrow" was left hanging on a comma: "But all remained unchanged,"[21]

And that comma, left up in the air, the rest of the story unknown, seems to open onto our future.

"The future is dark, which is the best thing the future can be, I think," wrote Virginia Woolf in her journal on January 18, 1915.[22] She was talking about herself (she was emerging from her veronal overdose), and she was talking about the world. There are dates we, the inhabitants of the future, know are not good dates. The year 1915—and Woolf is unaware that the darkness will last for three years, and two more if we count the Spanish Flu pandemic, and many years more if we count what will follow and what is simply the same sequence: "crisis," fascism, war ... But *dark* doesn't mean imprisoned. Only dark. We can get through the shadows in the present, step by step. Do away with nostalgia for the future, the famous future of "progress" that gleamed in my childhood, with its senseless promise of growth. Change the image of the future, even a tiny bit, shift ourselves ever so little, a small sidestep— that's what literature is for. An enormous ambition, and yet a modest one—in order to wake up slightly different.

And there, in those awakenings, perhaps in the bedroom, or with our forehead pressed against the window, or walking, seeking eye contact above masks, or encountering huge trees and other animals, we might find insomnia without fatigue, we might remember nights as a dimension of days.

Acknowledgments

My thanks to Lydie Arickx, Gilles Barbier, Nelly Blumenthal, Michel Caire, Emmanuel Charles, Claire Denis, Juliana Dorso, Didier Dutour, Charles Fréger, Rachid Hami, Fabrice Hyber, Adão Iturrusgarai, Emmelene Landon, Marcos Lutyens, Annette Messager, Riad Sattouf;

to Benjamin Abtan, Éric Aeschimann, Maud Barral, Hubertus Biermann, Yann Diener, Laurence Dodille, Marie Dumora, Laure Gouraige, Jonathan Hammer, Mary Horlock, Darian Leader, Camille Monduit de Caussade, Jamel Oubechou, Sylvie Royant-Parola, Lil Sclavo, Florence Tibout, Hayet Zeggar;

to Emmanuelle Touati.

Notes

Prologue

1. Michèle Manceaux, *Éloge de l'insomnie* (Paris: Hachette, 1985).

2. "There is nothing worse than being an insomniac in Buenos Aires." *Jorge Luis Borges: Conversations*, ed. Richard Burgin (Jackson: University of Mississippi, 1998).

3. The whole length of the Congo River "carries the country's insomnia in its belly." Tchicaya U Tam'si, *Le Ventre / Le Pain ou la Cendre* (Paris: Présence Africaine, 1978).

4. Franz Kafka, diary entry dated October 18, 1917, in *The Blue Octavo Notebooks*, ed. Max Brod, trans. Ernst Kaiser and Eithne Wilkins (Cambridge, MA: Exact Change, 1991).

5. E. M. Cioran, interview by Léo Gillet, in *Entretiens* (Paris: Gallimard, 1995).

6. Marcel Proust, *In Search of Lost Time*, vol. 1, *Swann's Way*, trans. C. K. Scott Moncrieff and Terence Kilmartin, rev. D. J. Enright (London: Chatto & Windus, 1992).

7. Ernest Hemingway, "A Clean, Well-Lighted Place," in *Winner Take Nothing* (New York: Charles Scribner's Sons, 1933).

I. The Deep Sleep in My Skull

1. Fernando Pessoa, "Insomnia," in *The Collected Poems of Álvaro de Campos*, vol. 2, *1928–1935*, trans. Chris Daniels (Exeter: Shearsman Books, 2009).

2. Jonah 1: 5–6 (King James Version).

3. Hélène Berr, *Journal* (Paris: Tallandier, 2008).

4. H. de Balzac, *Father Goriot (Le Père Goriot) and M. Gobseck*, trans. Ellen Marriage (Philadelphia: Gebbie, 1898). Vautrin, a character from Balzac's *The Human Comedy* series, likes to cite proverbs about sleep. In this instance he is under the influence of a sleeping draught that knocks him out.

5. Blaise Pascal, *Pensées*, trans. A. J. Krailsheimer (London: Penguin Books, 1986).

6. Matteo Maillard, "Au Mali, l'effondrement des transferts d'argent de la diaspora frappe durement les populations," *Le Monde*, April 30, 2020, https://www.lemonde.fr/afrique/article/2020/04/30/au-mali-l-effondrement-des-transferts-d-argent-de-la-diaspora-fragilise-gravement-les-populations_6038309_3212.html.

7. Pierre Reverdy, "La lucarne ovale," in *Plupart du temps: 1915–1922* (Paris: Poésie/Gallimard, 2004).

8. Violette Leduc, *Je hais les dormeurs* (Nolay, Fr.: Les éditions du Chemin de fer, 2006).

9. Marcel Proust, *In Search of Lost Time*, vol. 4, *Sodom and Gomorrah*, trans. C. K. Scott Moncrieff and Terence Kilmartin, rev. D. J. Enright (London: Chatto and Windus, 1992).

10. Manceaux, *Éloge de l'insomnie*.

11. Leonard Cohen, *The Favorite Game: A Novel* (New York: Vintage Books, 2003).

12. See Roland Barthes, *On Racine*, trans. Richard Howard (Berkeley: University of California Press, 1992).

13. Jean Racine, *Phaedra: A Verse Translation of Racine's Phèdre*, trans. Robert Lowell (London: Faber and Faber, 1971).

14. Émile Zola, *Germinal*, trans. Havelock Ellis (London: Everyman's Library, 1991).

15. Marie-Henri Beyle [Stendhal], *The Charterhouse of Parma*, trans. C. K. Scott Moncrieff (New York: Liveright, 1944).

16. Honoré de Balzac, *Lost Souls*, trans. Raymond N. MacKenzie (Minneapolis: University of Minnesota Press, 2021).

17. There were demonstrations between the classicists and the Romantics on the opening night of Hugo's play *Hernani* in 1830. See Jeanne Stranart, "L'interdiction de *Ruy Blas* et l'interruption d'*Hernani* en 1867, vues par Juliette Drouet," in *Correspondance et théâtre*, ed. Jean-Marc Hovasse (Rennes: Presses universitaires de Rennes, 2012); and Fanny Déchanet-Platz, "L'Insomnie créatrice chez Musset, Hugo, et Corbière," *Dix-Neuf: Journal of the Society of Dix-Neuviémistes* 16, no. 3 (2012).

18. Emmanuel Levinas, *Existence and Existents,* trans. Alphonso Lingis (Pittsburgh: Duquesne University Press, 2001).

19. Manceaux, *Éloge de l'insomnie.*

20. Madame de Sévigné, *Selected Letters*, trans. Leonard Tancock (London: Penguin Books, 1982).

21. Camille Vignes, "Césars 2020: L'actrice Sara Forestier exprime sa colère face à Polanski et ses prix," *Écran Large*, March 1, 2020, https://www.ecran-large.com/films/news/1166940-cesars-2020-lactrice-sara-forestier-exprime-sa-colere-face-a-polanski-et-ses-prix.

22. Frédéric Lemaître, "'Il ne faut pas diffuser cette information au public': L'échec du système de détection chinois face au coronavirus," *Le Monde*, April 6, 2020, https://www.lemonde.fr/international/article/2020/04/06/il-ne-faut-pas-diffuser-cette-information-au-public-l-echec-du-systeme-de-detection-chinois_6035704_3210.html.

23. Samantha Harvey, *The Shapeless Unease: A Year of Not Sleeping* (London: Jonathan Cape, 2020).

24. Euripides, *Électre / Oreste*, trans. Marie Delcourt-Curvers (Paris: Folio Théâtre, 2019).

25. Regulus is also the name of one of the brightest stars seen in the Northern Hemisphere, named by Copernicus after the tortured consul.

26. Joshua Wong, young prodemocracy activist in Hong Kong: "The light in my cell was kept on 24/7, I had to put a mask over my eyes to try and sleep." Wong seems to have extraordinary moral courage: "I needed a lot of time and energy to remain calm and to gather my wits," he said solemnly. *Le Monde*, December 3, 2020.

27. Jean-Baptiste Jacquin, "Une détenue de l'ETA embarrasse la justice française," *Le Monde*, October 30, 2019, https://www.lemonde.fr/societe/article/2019/10/30/une-detenue-de-l-eta-embarasse-la-justice-francaise_6017437_3224.html.

28. Alfred Dreyfus, *Five Years of My Life: The Diary of Captain Alfred Dreyfus*, trans. James Mortimer (New York: Peebles, 1977).

29. Franz Kafka, *Diaries, 1910–1923*, ed. Max Brod, trans. Joseph Kresh (New York: Schocken Books, 2000).

30. Cioran, interview by Gillet.

31. Emil Cioran, preface to *Sur les cimes du désespoir*, trans. André Vornic (Paris: L'Herne, 1990).

32. E. M. Cioran, *Notebooks*, trans. Richard Howard (New York: W. W. Norton, 2010).

33. Alix Cléo Roubaud, *Journal: 1979–1983* (Paris: Seuil, 1984).

34. Pessoa, "Insomnia."

35. Lyrics and music by Jarvis Cocker, Nicolas Godin, and Jean-Benoît Dunckel, from Gainsbourg's album of the same title (Because Music, 2006).

36. See Sarah Kane's emblematic play, and also her suicide letter, "4.48 Psychosis," in *Complete Plays* (London: Methuen, 2001).

37. Violette Leduc, *Ravages*, trans. D. Coltman (New York: HarperCollins, 1969).

38. Manceaux, *Éloge de l'insomnie*.

39. Christian Oster, *Les Rendez-vous* (Paris: Minuit, 2003).

40. F. Scott Fitzgerald, "Sleeping and Waking," in *The Crack-Up*, ed. Edmund Wilson (New York: New Directions, 1993).

41. Victor Hugo, "Insomnia," in *Selected Poems of Victor Hugo: A Bilingual Edition*, trans. E. H. and A. M. Blackmore (Chicago: University of Chicago Press, 2004).

42. Chinua Achebe, *Things Fall Apart* (New York: Anchor Books, 1994).

43. Georges Simenon, *Maigret and the Dead Girl*, trans. Howard Curtis (New York: Penguin Classics, 2017).

II. Searching for So Long

1. Tezer Özlü, *La vie hors du temps: Voyage sur les traces de Kafka, Svevo et Pavese*, trans. Diane Meur (Saint-Pourçain-sur-Sioule, Fr.: Bleu autour, 2014).

2. Franz Kafka, *Letters to Friends, Family, and Editors*, trans. Richard and Clara Winston (New York: Schocken Books, 1977).

3. Arthur Rimbaud, "Cities," in *Illuminations*, trans. John Ashbery (Manchester: Carcanet Classics, 2018).

4. Dominique Mabin, *Le sommeil de Marcel Proust* (Paris: Presses universitaires de France, 1992).

5. Paul Valéry, *The Outlook for Intelligence*, ed. Jackson Mathews, trans. Denise Folliot and Jackson Mathews (New York: Harper Torchbooks / Bollingen Library, 1962).

6. Ottessa Moshfegh, *My Year of Rest and Relaxation* (New York: Penguin Books, 2019).

7. Rainer Werner Fassbinder, *The Bitter Tears of Petra von Kant and Blood on the Neck of the Cat*, trans. Anthony Vivis (London: Amber Lane, 1984).

8. Peter Handke, *A Sorrow Beyond Dreams: A Life Story*, trans. Ralph Manheim (New York: Farrar, Straus and Giroux, 2012).

9. Sadeq Hedayat, *The Blind Owl*, trans. D. P. Costello (New York: Grove, 2012).

10. Natalie Levisalles, "A Posthumous Portrait of Césaire," *Libération*, April 18, 2008.

11. Cioran, *Notebooks*.

12. William Shakespeare, *Othello*, ed. Norman Sanders (Cambridge: Cambridge University Press, 2003).

13. During the last years of his life, all Proust ate was milky coffee and bits of croissant. At the end of his ordeal, the poor soul weighed no more than thirty-odd kilos.

14. This and all further quotes from Proust, unless otherwise indicated, are taken from Mabin, *Le sommeil de Marcel Proust*.

15. Céleste Albaret, *Monsieur Proust*, trans. Barbara Bray (New York: New York Review Books, 2003).

16. Proust writing to Rosny (the elder). In another letter, to Countess Greffulhe, he describes his insomnia as "an illness a lot like death."

17. Proust, *Swann's Way*.

18. Albaret, *Monsieur Proust*.

19. Céleste Albaret, *Monsieur Proust* (Paris: Robert Laffont, 1973).

20. Fanny Déchanet-Platz, "Les risques de l'insomnie," in *L'Écrivain, le sommeil et les rêves: 1800–1945* (Paris: Gallimard, 2008).

21. Mabin, *Le sommeil de Marcel Proust*.

22. Jacques Dutronc, "Berceuse," from the album *33 Ans De Travail, vol. 2, Les Années 80–90* (Columbia, 1998).

23. David Labreure, "Louis Ferdinand Céline: Une pensée médicale" (DEA thesis, Université Paris 1 Panthéon-Sorbonne, 2005), https://www.memoire-online.com/06/07/482/m_louis-ferdinand-celine-une-pensee-medicale.html.

24. Roubaud, *Journal*.

25. See Viviane Forrester, *Virginia Woolf: A Portrait*, trans. Jody Gladding (New York: Columbia University Press, 2015).

26. Marcel Proust, letter to Nathalie Barney, end of November 1920, in *Correspondance de Marcel Proust*, vol. 19, *1920*, ed. Philip Kolb (Paris: Plon, 1970).

27. Marcel Proust, letter to Maurice Duplay, in Duplay's *Mon ami Marcel Proust: Souvenirs intimes* (Paris: Gallimard, 1972). In *Monsieur Proust*, Céleste Albaret goes further: "His book was his god and his determination to finish it was far too great to interrupt his writing in order to kill himself."

28. Kenzaburō Ōe, *Ōe Kenzaburō, l'écrivain par lui-même: Entretiens avec Ozaki Mariko*, trans. Corinne Quentin (Arles Cedex, Fr.: Philippe Picquier, 2014).

29. Kenzaburō Ōe, *A Personal Matter*, trans. John Nathan (New York: Grove, 1969).

30. Ryūnosuke Akutagawa, "A Note to a Certain Old Friend," trans. Beongcheon Yu, in *The Essential Akutagawa: Rashomon, Hell Screen, Cogwheels, A Fool's Life and Other Short Fiction*, ed. Seiji M. Lippit (New York: Marsilio, 1999), emphasis added. The phrase can also be translated, according to my friend Masayo Nomura, as "obscure fear," or, according to my Japanese translator, as "vague insecurity"; anyway, we get the idea.

31. Ryūnosuke Akutagawa, *The Life of a Stupid Man*, trans. Jay Rubin (London: Penguin Classics, 2015).

32. Cesare Pavese, *This Business of Living: Diaries 1939–1950*, trans. A. E. Murch (London: Routledge, 2009).

33. Amy Liptrot, *The Outrun: A Memoir* (New York: W. W. Norton, 2017).

34. Louise Erdrich, *Shadow Tag* (New York: Harper, 2010).

35. Pierre Fouquet, a French physician and pioneer in alcohology, came up with this definition in 1955.

36. Laure Adler, *Marguerite Duras: A Life* (London: Victor Gollancz, 2000); I am also drawing here from stories Paul Otchakovsky-Laurens told me about "Marguerite."

37. Manceaux, *Éloge de l'insomnie*.

38. Carole Angier, afterword to *Voyage in the Dark*, by Jean Rhys (London: Penguin, 2000).

39. Lawrence Durrell, *A Smile in the Mind's Eye* (London: Wildwood House, 1980).

40. From a personal conversation, ca. 1997.

41. Alexander Pushkin, *Eugene Onegin: A Novel in Verse*, trans. James E. Falen (Oxford: Oxford University Press, 1998).

42. On June 15, 2020, baclofen was officially approved in France for use in the treatment of alcoholism, but in very weak doses (80 mg per day). On June 18, the license was suspended. On November 25, the Council of State annulled the suspension.

43. Olivier Ameisen, the doctor who identified baclofen's effect on the compulsive desire to consume alcohol, said that the drug also released him from the panic attacks connected to withdrawal. Olivier Ameisen, *The End of My Addiction: How One Man Cured Himself of Alcoholism* (London: Piatkus, 2010).

44. Thomas de Quincey, *Thomas De Quincey's Works*, vol. 3, *Last Days of Immanuel Kant and other Writings* (Edinburgh: Adam and Charles Black, 1871).

45. Henri Michaux, "Dormir," in *Œuvres complètes*, vol. 1, ed. Raymond Bellour (Paris: Bibliothèque de la Pléiade,1998).

46. Georges Perec, *A Void*, trans. Gilbert Adair (London: Harvill, 1994).

47. Georges Perec, *Life: A User's Manual*, trans. David Bellos (London: Vintage, 2003).

48. Lisa Halliday, *Asymmetry* (New York: Simon and Schuster, 2018).

49. Joris-Karl Huysmans, *Against Nature*, ed. Nicholas White, trans. Margaret Mauldon (Oxford: Oxford University Press, 2009).

50. André Gide, journal entry, December 1921, in *Journals*, vol. 2, *1914–1927*, trans. Justin O'Brien (Urbana: University of Illinois Press, 2000).

51. Mari Akasaka, *Vibrator*, trans. Michael Emmerich (London: Faber and Faber, 2005).

52. Michaux, *Œuvres completes*.

53. Ernest Hemingway, "Now I Lay Me," in *Men without Women* (New York: Charles Scribner's Sons, 1927).

54. Antoine Bertrand, *Les curiosités esthétiques de Robert de Montesquiou*, vol. 1 (Geneva: Librairie Droz, 1996).

55. William Shakespeare, *Hamlet, Prince of Denmark*, ed. Philip Edwards (Cambridge: Cambridge University Press, 2012).

56. Homer, *The Iliad of Homer*, trans. Richmond Lattimore (Chicago: University of Chicago Press, 2011).

57. Xavier de Maistre, *Voyage around My Room*, trans. Stephen Sartarelli (New York: New Directions, 2016). Maistre's *Expédition nocturne autour de ma chamber* (*Nocturnal Expedition around My Room*), finished in 1825, is the lesser known and darker sequel to the hedonistic *Voyage autour de ma chambre*

(*Voyage around My Room*, 1794), both of which Éditions Sillage had the excellent idea to republish in May 2020, at the end of the first lockdown in France.

58. Hedayat, *The Blind Owl*. "[My room] has a whitewashed interior with a strip of inscription. It is exactly like a grave."

59. François Roustang makes a distinction between restricted wakefulness, which is our normal state of consciousness, and the generalized wakefulness of hypnosis, which allows us to access a world that is more immense, more dreamlike, more imaginary, close to psychosis and to poetry. The state of hypnosis is "a retreat from the outside world that is accompanied by a rise in capacity of one's personal life." François Roustang, *What Is Hypnosis?*, trans. Anna Vila (n.p.: Versilio, 2019), EPUB.

It seems to me that insomnia, on the good nights, is a form of self-hypnosis; it is literally, yes, "a retreat from the outside world that is accompanied by a rise in capacity of one's personal life," cut off from the demands of a socially vigilant ego. The mental domain that emerges is conducive to writing; it's "just" that the cost in fatigue is enormous …

60. Marie Darrieussecq, *A Brief Stay with the Living*, trans. Ian Monk (London: Faber and Faber, 2003).

61. Aldo Leopold, *A Sand County Almanac and Sketches Here and There* (New York: Oxford University Press, 1949).

62. Frigyes Karinthy, *A Journey round My Skull*, trans. Vernon Duckworth Barker (New York: New York Review Books, 2008).

III. Zones, Abysses, Ravines

1. Ovid, "To Flaccus," *Ex Ponto*, bk. 1, letter 10, in *Tristia, Ex Ponto*, trans. Arthur Leslie Wheeler, (Cambridge, MA: Harvard University Press, 1939).

2. Peter Handke, *The Jukebox and Other Essays on Storytelling*, trans. Ralph Manheim (New York: Farrar, Straus and Giroux, 1994).

3. Dino Buzzati, *The Tartar Steppe*, trans. Stuart C. Hood (London: Secker and Warburg, 1952).

4. Maistre, *Voyage around My Room*.

5. See Julio Cortázar, "Continuity of Parks," trans. Alberto Manguel, in *Bestiary: Selected Stories* (New York: Penguin Random House, 2020)—a short story in the form of a feedback loop, first published in Spanish in 1964.

6. Kafka, *Diaries, 1910–1923*.

7. Clément Rosset, *Route de nuit: Épisodes cliniques* (Paris: Gallimard, 1999).

8. Kafka, *Diaries, 1910–1923*.

9. Lyrics from Alain Bashung's "La nuit je mens," on his album *Fantaisie militiare* (Universal Music, 1998). The most beautiful song in the world.

10. Barbara, "Les Insomnies," from the album *CD Story* (Polygram, 2000); and Pomme, "Ceux qui rêvent," from the album *À peu près* (Polydor, 2017).

11. Levinas, *Existence and Existents*.

12. Handke, *A Sorrow beyond Dreams*.

13. The title is impossible today. You have to read this novel, written in 1897, in order to understand that Conrad is denouncing racism, and that it is one of his most beautiful pieces of writing.

14. Nikolaj Frobenius, *Je est ailleurs*, trans. Lena Grumbach and Hélène Hervieu (Arles: Actes Sud, 2004).

15. Christopher Nolan's 2002 film is a remake of the Norwegian original, directed by Erik Skoldbjærg, with the same screenwriter.

16. Adolfo Bioy Casares, *The Invention of Morel*, trans. Suzanne Jill Levine (New York: New York Review Books, 2004). Casaras was Borges's best friend in Buenos Aires.

17. Edgar Allan Poe, "The Premature Burial," in *Complete Works of Edgar Allan Poe*, vol. 5, *Tales* (New York: Fred de Fau, 1902).

18. Niki de Saint Phalle, *Traces: An Autobiography* (Lausanne: Acatos, 2000).

19. De Quincey, *Last Days of Immanuel Kant*.

20. Albaret, *Monsieur Proust*.

21. For a long time I thought these were Stanislaw Lem's words, but I have just reread the whole novel (because I'm an insomniac) and they're not there. In fact, it was in Tarkovsky's film adaptation that I heard this (or rather read it in the subtitles). This addition summarizes the whole novel and improves it. It is because this novel is both brilliant and flawed that it allows so much room for film versions: Tarkovsky in 1972, Soderbergh in 2002 (with George Clooney as Kelvin), Ryûsuke Hamaguchi in 2007.

22. Kafka, *Diaries, 1910–1923*.

23. Ōe, *A Personal Matter*.

24. Marie Darrieussecq, *Crossed Lines*, trans. Penny Hueston (Melbourne: Text Publishing, 2020).

25. Directed by Oren Peli, 2009.

26. "Le courage des oiseaux" (The courage of birds) is the title of a song by Dominique A., who, I believe, left a lasting impression on my generation with his album *Un disque sourd* (self-released, 1991).

27. Vincent Ravalec, Mallendi, and Agnès Paicheler, *Iboga: The Visionary Root of African Shamanism* (Rochester, VT: Park Street, 2007).

28. Pierre Éric Mbog Batassi, "Gabon-Sorcellerie: D'horribles fétiches retrouvés dans une maison à Libreville," Afrik.com, April 28, 2014, https://www.afrik.com/gabon-sorcellerie-d-horribles-fetiches-retrouves-dans-une-maison-a-libreville.

29. Ovid, *Metamorphoses*, bk. 10, lines 53–54, translation by Michael Heyward.

30. Andrea Schutz, "Ovid," in *From Polis to Empire—The Ancient World, c. 800 B.C.–A.D. 500; A Biographical Dictionary*, ed. Andrew G. Traver (Westport, CT: Greenwood, 2002).

31. Ovid, *Letters from the Black Sea*, bk. 1, letter 10, lines 21–23, translation by Michael Heyward.

32. Ibid., bk. 3, letter 1, lines 19–23, translation by Michael Heyward.

33. Ovid, *Sorrows*, bk. 3, letter 3, line 37, translation by Michael Heyward.

34. Ibid., lines 62–66, translation by Michael Heyward.

35. Ibid., bk. 3, letter 9, lines 33–34, translation by Michael Heyward.

36. Ovid, *Letters from the Black Sea*, bk. 3, letter 3, lines 11–12, translation by Michael Heyward.

IV. "Everyone Carries a Room About inside Them"

1. Kafka, *The Blue Octavo Notebooks*.

2. Henri Michaux, "The Night Moves," in *Darkness Moves: An Henri Michaux Anthology, 1927–1984*, ed. and trans. David Ball (Berkeley: University of California Press, 1994).

3. William Styron, *Darkness Visible: A Memoir of Madness* (New York: Random House, 1990).

4. Michelle Perrot, *The Bedroom: An Intimate History*, trans. Lauren Elkin (New Haven, CT: Yale University Press, 2018). "Keeping to one's room" has become topical again during pandemic lockdowns and isolations.

5. Sleeping in separate rooms is "the last taboo of the couple," according to Jean-Paul Kaufman in his book *Un lit pour deux: La tendre guerre* (Paris: Lattès, 2015). "No one wants to hear that it might only be a technical issue to do with sleeping conditions." Jean-Paul Kaufman, "La chambre à part, dernier tabou du couple," interview by Pascale Kremer, https://www.lemonde.fr/m-perso/article/2015/01/07/la-chambre-a-part-dernier-tabou-du-couple_4550925_4497916.html.

6. Perrot, *The Bedroom*.

7. Andrey Tarkovsky, *Time within Time: The Diaries, 1970–1986*, trans. Kitty Hunter-Blair (Kolkata: Seagull Books, 2019).

8. Colette, *The Other One*, trans. Elizabeth Tait and Roger Senhouse (New York: Farrar, Straus and Giroux, 1960).

9. This was particularly true during lockdown, as shown by the statistics on domestic violence. As the pediatrician and psychoanalyst Françoise Dolto says, parents have to leave the room when there is mounting violence against a child.

10. James Knowlson, *Damned to Fame: The Life of Samuel Beckett* (New York: Grove Press, 2004). All references are to this edition.

11. Simone Boué, interview by Norbert Dodille, in *Lectures de Cioran*, ed. Norbert Dodille and Gabriel Liiceanu (Paris: L'Harmattan, 1997).

12. Maistre, *Voyage around My Room*.

13. Violette Leduc, *Ravages* (Paris: Gallimard, 1955).

14. Because of his green bedcover; see Walter Benjamin, "A Berlin Chronicle," in *Reflections: Essays, Aphorisms, Autobiographical Writings*, ed. Peter Demetz, trans. Edmund Jephcott (New York: Harcourt Brace Jovanovich, 1978).

15. Georges Perec, *Species of Spaces and Other Pieces*, trans. John Sturrock (London: Penguin Books, 2008).

16. Georges Perec, *Things: A Story of the '60s with A Man Asleep*, trans. Andrew Leak (London: Collins Harvill, 1990).

17. Brigitte Fontaine, "Il se passe des choses," from the album *Brigitte Fontaine est… folle!* (Saravah, 1968).

18. Michaux, "Peintures," in *Œuvres complètes*, vol. 1.

19. Proust, *Swann's Way*.

20. Cioran, *Notebooks*.

21. Rhys, *Voyage in the Dark*.

22. Roubaud, *Journal*.

23. Carlo Amedeo Reyneri di Lagnasco, *Feng Shui: Viento y agua* (Paris: De Vecchi, 1999).

24. Karen Kingston, *Clear Your Clutter with Feng Shui* (London: Piatkus, 2016).

25. Di Lagnasco, *Feng Shui*.

26. Lyrics from the song "Foule sentimentale" by Alain Souchon, on his album *C'est déjà ça* (Virgin, 1993).

27. Razmig Keucheyan, *Les Besoins artificiels: Comment sortir du consumérisme* (Paris: La Découverte, 2019).

28. Marie Kondo, *The Life-Changing Magic of Tidying Up: The Japanese Art of Decluttering and Organizing* (Berkeley: Ten Speed Press, 2014).

29. See Freyer's website for this project, http://www.allmylifeforsale.com. Freyer also published a book of photos, *All My Life for Sale* (London: Bloomsbury, 2002).

30. Benjamin, "A Berlin Chronicle."

31. Thomas Bernhard, *Woodcutters*, trans. David McLintock (New York: Alfred A. Knopf, 1987); and *The Loser*, trans. Jack Dawson (New York: Alfred A. Knopf, 1991).

32. Samuel Beckett, "First Love," in *First Love and Other Shorts* (New York: Grove, 1974).

33. Albaret, *Monsieur Proust*.

34. You can see all the hotels I've stayed in on my website, https://mariedarrieussecq.com.

35. *It Follows* is the title of a wonderful 2014 horror movie written and directed by David Robert Mitchell.

36. Perrot, *The Bedroom*.

37. Aeschylus, *The House of Atreus: Being the Agamemnon, Libation-Bearers, and Furies of Æschylus*, trans. E. D. A. Morshead (London: C. Kegan Paul, 1881).

38. Levinas, *Existence and Existents*.

39. Fitzgerald, "Sleeping and Waking."

40. Simenon, *Maigret and the Dead Girl*.

41. Françoise Frenkel, *A Bookshop in Berlin: The Rediscovered Memoir of One Woman's Harrowing Escape from the Nazis*, trans. Stephanie Smee (New York: Atria Books, 2019).

42. Patrick Modiano, preface to *A Bookshop in Berlin*, by Frenkel.

43. Franz Kafka, *The Castle*, trans. J. A. Underwood (London: Penguin, 1997).

44. Ibid.

45. Didier Fassin, Alain Morice, and Catherine Quiminal, *Les Lois de l'inhospitalité: Les politiques de l'immigration à l'épreuve des sans-papiers* (Paris: La Découverte, 1997).

V. A World of Networks and Vines

1. Grégoire Solotareff, *Le Masque* (Paris: L'Ecole des loisirs, 2001). This picture book was the source of gleeful terror for my children at bedtime.

2. See A. Roger Ekirch, *At Day's Close: A History of Nighttime* (London: Weidenfeld and Nicolson, 2006).

3. See *La Fabrique de l'Histoire*, special series, "Une histore de la nuit," episode 4, "Qu'était la nuit avant l'éclairage public?," produced by Emmanuel Laurentin, aired March 20, 2008, on Radio France, https://www.radiofrance.fr/franceculture/podcasts/la-fabrique-de-l-histoire/qu-etait-la-nuit-avant-l-eclairage-public-4810610.

4. Liam Tung, "Microsoft: Azure Delays Not Acknowledged for 5 Hours Because Manager Was Asleep," ZDNet, April 9, 2020, https://www.zdnet.com/article/microsoft-azure-delays-not-acknowledged-for-5-hours-because-manager-was-asleep/.

5. His photo circulated widely, many celebrating his nap as "an act of resistance": see, for example, Amy Walker, "Boy Named Trump Who Fell Asleep During State of the Union Hailed a Hero," *Guardian*, February 6, 2019, https://www.theguardian.com/us-news/2019/feb/06/the-trump-who-fell-asleep-during-state-of-the-union-hailed-a-hero.

6. Jacques Rouxel, *Les Shadoks: Pompe à rebours* (Paris: Grasset, 1975).

7. Paul Gadenne, "Insomnie," in *Scènes dans le château* (Paris: Actes Sud, 1986).

8. Franz Kafka, "In the Penal Colony," in *Konundrum: Selected Prose of Franz Kafka*, ed. and trans. Peter Wortsman (Brooklyn, NY: Archipelago Books, 2016).

9. Stefan Zweig, *The World of Yesterday: Memoirs of a European*, trans. Anthea Bell (London: Pushkin, 2011).

10. Stefan Zweig, "The Sleepless World," in *Messages from a Lost World: Europe on the Brink*, trans. Will Stone (London: Pushkin, 2016).

11. For the first lockdown, see Li-yu Lin et al., "The Immediate Impact of the 2019 Novel Coronavirus (COVID-19) Outbreak on Subjective Sleep Status," *Sleep Medicine* 77 (January 2021), https://doi.org/10.1016/j.sleep.2020.05.018. For the second lockdown, see Institut National du Sommeil et de la Vigilance, "Bien dormir pour mieux faire face," press release for Journée du Sommeil 2021, March 16, 2021, https://institut-sommeil-vigilance.org/wp-content/uploads/2020/02/CP_JS2021_vdef.pdf. According to this survey, 45 percent of French people reported sleeping difficulties during the lockdown, compared to 41 percent in normal times. Additionally, 26 percent of French people reported decreased quality of sleep, in particular young people aged 18–24 (39 percent) and the 27 percent of French people who worked exclusively remotely, or who didn't work, during this period. Conversely, people gained sleep time by not commuting.

12. Fang Fang, *Wuhan Diary: Dispatches from a Quarantined City*, trans. Michael Berry (New York: HarperVia, 2020).

13. Pascal, *Pensées*.

14. As Mona Chollet writes, "Because of the internet, it is rare to experience that restorative, enriching impression of a change of scenery that homebodies have in their own domestic space." *Chez soi: Une odyssée de l'espace domestique* (Paris: Zone, 2015).

15. Yevgeny Zamyatin, *We*, trans. Mirra Ginsburg (New York: Avon Books, 1987). The novel was written in 1920, but the new Soviet Union forbade publication.

16. Charlotte Beradt, *The Third Reich of Dreams: The Nightmares of a Nation 1933–1939*, trans. Adriane Gottwald (Wellingborough, UK: Aquarian, 1985).

17. Gustaw Herling, *Volcano and Miracle: A Selection from The Journal Written at Night*, trans. Ronald Strom (New York: Penguin Books, 1997).

18. There are a lot of serious studies on the issue of Dante's narcolepsy: see, for example, Giuseppe Plazzi, "Dante's Description of Narcolepsy," *Sleep Medicine* 14, no. 11 (November 2013), https://doi.org/10.1016/j.sleep.2013.07.005; or Francesco Maria Galassi, Michael E. Habicht, and Frank J. Rühli, "Dante Alighieri's Narcolepsy," *Lancet Neurology* 15, no. 3 (March 2016), https://doi.org/10.1016/S1474-4422(16)00029-6. Fortunately, *The Divine Comedy* cannot be reduced to a diagnosis.

19. Marie Darrieussecq, *Men*, trans. Penny Hueston (Melbourne: Text Publishing, 2016).

20. Benjamin, "A Berlin Chronicle."

21. Pushkin, *Eugene Onegin*.

22. "In 2001, Henri Nleme, the Bagheli representative for Campo Ma'an, had this to say: 'Do you know why there are no more animals in the forest? If you do, tell me why. Me, all I know is that if the animals are fleeing from the forest, it is because there are people who cut down the fruit trees they need to feed themselves. Before, there was only one road to Campo. Even I, I could not go to Campo, there was nothing but forests. There were all kinds of animals: elephants, gorillas, and so many other species. Now that people have begun to exploit the forest, all the trees have been destroyed, there is a lot of noise, there are people who hunt with firearms—and the animals have disappeared. Now, it is just a deserted place. It is those using guns that have killed the most animals. We, we use only nets, dogs, and assegai spears. Nyabisen is the only place where one still finds animals. On the other bank of the Ntem, they do not let us hunt. If we are obliged to hunt around the houses, what can we catch? I do not understand why they tell us to stop hunting. What will we do to survive?'" Marie Darrieussecq, "The Other Animals," *Passa Porta*, March 24, 2021, https://www.passaporta.be/en/magazine/invoer-109896.

23. Mary Kingsley, *Travels in West Africa* (Washington, DC: National Geographic, 2002).

24. The video is on my website, under the "UNIVERS" tab on the page for *Il faut beaucoup aimer les hommes*: https://mariedarrieussecq.com/livre/il-faut-beaucoup-aimer-les-hommes.

25. Louis-Ferdinand Céline, *Journey to the End of the Night*, trans. Ralph Manheim (New York: New Directions, 1983).

VI. End Up Sleeping?

1. "Feeling Good," by Anthony Newley and Leslie Bricusse, recorded by Simone for her album *I Put a Spell on You* (Philips, 1965).

2. Proust, *Swann's Way*.

3. In the first half of the twentieth century, many young women made the annual autumn trek on foot from Spain into French Basque towns to get work, often in espadrilles factories.

4. See Botho Strauss, *Three Plays*, trans. Jeremy Sams (London: Oberon Books, 2017).

5. I am the patron of the DES Network in France, an association that supports and provides information for victims of diethylstilbestrol, who number about

160,000 in France. A third of the "DES daughters" are infertile and have an increased risk of cancer. The teratogenic effects of diethylstilbestrol were already known in the 1950s; it was prohibited in Canada and the United States in 1971, but continued to be prescribed in France until 1977. See https://www.des-france.org/.

6. Marie Darrieussecq, *The Baby*, trans. Penny Hueston (Melbourne: Text Publishing, 2019).

7. Manceaux, *Éloge de l'insomnie*.

8. Jacques Rigaut, untitled essay ("I will be serious …"), in *Anthology of Black Humor*, ed. André Breton, trans. Mark Polizzotti (San Francisco: City Lights, 1997).

9. Jean-Yves Jouannais, *Artistes sans œuvres: I Would Prefer Not To* (Paris: Verticales, 2009).

10. A health network devoted to tackling sleep problems; see https://reseau-morphee.fr/.

11. A popular character in French crime fiction, invented in 1911.

12. Zamyatin, *We*.

13. "Irene is at great cost conveyed to Epidaurus; she visits Aesculapius in his temple and consults him about all her ailments. She complains first that she is weary and excessively fatigued, and the god replies that the long journey she just made is the cause of this; she says that she is not inclined to eat any supper, and the oracle orders her to eat less dinner; she adds she cannot sleep at night, and he prescribes her not to lie a-bed by day; she complains of her corpulency, and asks how it can be prevented; the oracle replies she should get up before noon and now and then use her legs to walk." Jean de La Bruyère's portrait of "The Hypochondriac" (I know), in *The Characters*, trans. Henri van Laun (London: Ballantyne Press, 1885).

14. Ovid, *Sorrows*, bk. 1, letter 11, lines 35–38, translation by Michael Heyward.

15. Ibid., lines 39–40, translation by Michael Heyward.

16. She is the one who recommended that I read A. Roger Ekirch's *At Day's Close*, which I mentioned earlier.

17. For the famous concept of "sleep debt" and the guilt associated with it, see Darian Leader's *Why Can't We Sleep?* (London: Penguin, 2019).

18. Michel de Montaigne, "Of Experience," in *The Complete Essays of Montaigne*, trans. Donald M. Frame (Stanford: Stanford University Press, 1965).

19. So many cases fall under the "destructive logic of a voluntary initiative" in which the "attempt to put in place a solution guarantees, in proportion to the agreed-upon effort, that the problem to resolve will persist." That's how Romain Graziani describes this "farce" in his book *L'Usage du vide: Essai sur l'intelligence de l'action, de l'Europe à la Chine* (Paris: Gallimard, 2019).

20. Boris Pasternak, *Doctor Zhivago*, trans. Richard Pevear and Larissa Volokhonsky (New York: Vintage, 2011).

21. Roustang, *What Is Hypnosis?*.

22. Ibid.

VII. Insomnia Nights

1. Paul Celan, "Sleep and Nourishment," in *Memory Rose Into Threshold Speech: The Collected Earlier Poetry*, trans. Pierre Joris (New York: Farrar, Straus and Giroux, 2020).

2. Kafka, "The Metamorphosis," trans. Willa and Edwin Muir, in *The Complete Stories* (New York: Schocken, 1983).

3. Marie-Caroline Saglio-Yatzimirsky, *La Voix de ceux qui crient: Rencontre avec des demandeurs d'asile* (Paris: Albin Michel, 2018).

4. "I shut my eyes. They're there. I open them, they're there." Coco, a survivor of the *Charlie Hebdo* attacks, in her beautiful graphic-novel account, *Dessiner encore* (Paris: Les Arènes BD, 2021).

5. Hemingway, "Now I Lay Me."

6. Zweig, *The World of Yesterday*.

7. Kafka, *Diaries, 1910–1923*.

8. André Breton, "Manifesto of Surrealism," in *Manifestoes of Surrealism*, trans. Richard Seaver and Helen R. Lane (Ann Arbor: University of Michigan Press, 1972).

9. Perec, *A Void*.

10. Elie Wiesel, *Night*, trans. Marion Wiesel (New York: Farrar, Straus and Giroux, 1958).

11. Primo Levi, *If This Is a Man*, trans. Stuart Woolf (London: Orion Press, 1959).

12. Robert Antelme, *The Human Race*, trans. Jeffrey Haight and Annie Mahler (Evanston, IL: Marlboro Press, 1998).

13. Charlotte Delbo, *Auschwitz and After*, trans. Rosette C. Lamont (New Haven, CT: Yale University Press, 1995).

14. Aharon Appelfeld, *The Man Who Never Stopped Sleeping*, trans. Jeffrey M. Green (New York: Schocken, 2020).

VIII. Other Bodies

1. Tarkovsky, *Time within Time*.

2. Primo Levi, "Other People's Trades," trans. Antony Shugaar, in *The Complete Works of Primo Levi*, vol. 3, ed. Ann Goldstein (New York: Liveright, 2015).

3. And it's probably time, in 2020, to sidestep again in our description of the world, and to say that we are on this planet with *other* animals. It's not the case that there are "animals" on one side, and then us. As Baptiste Morizot says about this "other," "It's a quiet grammatical revolution that's happening." "A very small adjective, so elegant in its cartographic reconfiguration of the world: it alone reframes both a logic of difference and a common belonging." Baptiste Morizot, *Ways of Being Alive*, trans. Andrew Brown (Medford, MA: Polity, 2021).

4. Jean-Christophe Bailly, *The Animal Side*, trans. Catherine Porter (New York: Fordham University Press, 2011).

5. Eduardo Kohn, *How Forests Think: Toward an Anthropology beyond the Human* (Berkeley: University of California Press, 2013).

6. Comte de Lautréamont, *The Songs of Maldoror*, trans. R. J. Dent (Chicago: University of Chicago Press, 2011).

7. Julio Cortázar, "Axolotl," in *End of the Game and Other Stories*, trans. Paul Blackburn (New York: Harper and Row, 1978).

8. Donna J. Haraway, *Simians, Cyborgs, and Women: The Reinvention of Nature* (New York: Routledge, 2013).

9. Aldo Leopold, *A Sand County Almanac & Other Writings on Ecology and Conservation* (New York: Library of America, 2013).

10. Élisabeth de Fontenay, *Without Offending Humans: A Critique of Animal Rights*, trans. Will Bishop (Minneapolis: University of Minnesota Press, 2012).

11. Leopold, *A Sand County Almanac*.

12. Olga Tokarczuk, *Drive Your Plow Over the Bones of the Dead*, trans. Antonia Lloyd-Jones (Melbourne: Text Publishing, 2018).

13. A reference to the lyrics of a famous song by the French singer Jacques Brel, "Ne Me Quitte Pas," from his album *No. 4* (Philips, 1959).

14. Isaac Bashevis Singer, "The Letter Writer," in *Collected Stories* (New York: Farrar, Straus and Giroux, 1996).

15. Later, other writers pushed me out of my familiar territory, out of my *bed*: Bruno Latour, Philippe Descola, Donna J. Haraway, Tim Ingold, Émilie Hache, Vinciane Despret, Baptiste Morizot, and others.

16. Midnight Oil, "Beds Are Burning," from the album *Diesel and Dust* (Columbia, 1987).

17. Colette, *The Other One*.

18. Nikolaj Frobenius, *Dark Branches*, trans. Frank Stewart (Dingwall, Scot.: Sandstone, 2015).

19. Akasaka, *Vibrator*.

20. Kafka, *Diaries, 1910–1923*.

21. Kafka, "The Burrow," trans. Willa and Edwin Muir, in *The Complete Stories*.

22. Rebecca Solnit wrote a brilliant commentary on this sentence in her essay "Woolf's Darkness: Embracing the Inexplicable," in *Men Explain Things to Me* (Chicago: Haymarket Books, 2015).

Image Credits

p. 12: Giotto, *Jonas Swallowed Up by the Whale*. Scrovegni Chapel (Arena Chapel), Padua.

p. 16: Françoise Pétrovitch, *Étendu* (Stretched out) or *Jeune fille allongée* (Young reclining woman). Screenshot from the video *Panorama*, directed by Pétrovitch in collaboration with Hervé Plumet, 2016. © 2021 by ADAGP, Paris.

p. 19: Riad Sattouf, *Les Cahiers d'Esther: Histoires de mes 15 ans* (Paris: Allary, 2021), 7.

p. 21: William Turner, *Regulus*, 1828. Oil on canvas, 89.5 × 123.8 cm. Photo © by the Tate Museum, London.

pp. 22–23: Alfred Dreyfus, *Cahiers de l'île du diable* (Paris: Artulis, 2009); facsimile edition based on the original manuscript held at the Bibliothèque nationale de France.

p. 25: Annette Messager, *Petite danse du matin* (Little morning dance), 2020. © 2021 by ADAGP, Paris.

p. 32: My stash. Photo by M. D.

p. 37: Céleste Albaret Albaret, *Monsieur Proust* (Paris: Robert Laffont, 1973).

p. 41: Insomniac selfie. Photo by Nicolas Fargues.

p. 45: Veronal. Rights reserved.

p. 47: Emmanuel Charles, *Dessin de rêve* (Dream drawing), 2020. © by Emmanuel Charles.

p. 52: Screenshot of Lloyd, the barman, from *The Shining*, dir. Stanley Kubrick. © 1980 by Warner Brothers Entertainment Inc.

p. 55: Ovid's Tears. Rights reserved.

p. 63: Juliana Dorso, *Portrait de R. endormie* (Portrait of R. sleeping), 2020. © by Juliana Dorso (@dorsojuliana).

p. 64: Henri Guérard, *Count Robert de Montesquiou-Fezensac*. Engraving, after Whistler (1st state, 2 prints, no. 1). © by Gallica, Bibliothèque nationale de France.

p. 67: Gilles Barbier *Squeezed Head*, 2010. Resin, 58 × 38 × 36 cm. Private collection; courtesy Galerie Georges-Philippe & Nathalie Vallois, Paris. Rights reserved.

p. 71: Marcos Lutyens, *The Reflection Room* in *Hypnotic Show*, dOCUMENTA 13, Kassel, 2012.

p. 74: The Morphée box. Photo by M. D.

p. 75: Champ de Fleurs mat. Photo by M. D.

p. 78: Particle accelerator, IGLIAS, GANIL-CIMAP platform, Caen, France.

p. 83: Yann Diener, *Ruban de Möbius* (Möbius strip). © by Yann Diener.

p. 84: Marie Darrieussecq, sketch from *Naissance des fantômes* (Paris: P.O.L., 1998).

p. 85: Emmelene Landon-Otchakovsky, *Naufrage* (Shipwreck), 2010. © by Emmelene Landon-Otchakovsky.

p. 88: Screenshot of Agata Buzek in *High Life*, dir. Claire Denis, 2018. © by Alcatraz Films.

p. 89: Illustration of pilot fish from Francis Day's *The Fishes of India*, vol. 2 (London: Bernard Quaritch, 1878).

p. 92: Niki de Saint Phalle, "Insomnia," a poem from *Traces: An Autobiography* (Lausanne: Acatos, 2000).

p. 93: Screenshot of the space station in *Solaris*, dir. Andrei Tarkovsky, 1972. © by Mosfilm, Russia.

p. 98 (*top*): Amaxi. Rights reserved.

p. 98 (*bottom*): My great-great-aunt. Rights reserved.

p. 99: Marie Darrieussecq, sketch from *Naissance des fantômes* (Paris: P.O.L., 1998).

p. 101: Charles Fréger, *La Suite basque, Exiliados* (The Basque suite, the exiled), 2015–16. © by Charles Fréger.

p. 102: Saint Michael unsheathing his sword. Photo by M. D.

p. 103: Elephants in Gabon. Photo by M. D.

p. 107: Constanza Tree. Photo by M. D.

p. 110: Abandoned room, Chernobyl Exclusion Zone. Photo by M. D.

p. 112: Isolation rooms. Photos by Rachid Hami.

p. 116: De Beauvoir and Sartre's plaque. Photo by M. D.

p. 118: Illustration of beds from the *Larousse Universel* encyclopedia (Paris: Librairie Larousse, 1922).

p. 119: Children's cubby-house. Photo © 2020 by Nelly Blumenthal.

p. 122: Marcel Proust's bed, maker unknown, ca. 1880. Musée Carnavalet, Paris.

p. 128: Gilles Barbier, *Le Terrier* (The burrow), 2005. Mixed media, 420 × 250 × 300 cm. Installation view of the exhibition *Gilles Barbier: Machines de production* (Gilles Barbier: Production machines), Soulages Museum, Rodez, 2021. © by Christian Bousquet. Courtesy Galerie Georges-Philippe & Nathalie Vallois, Paris. Photo by Thierry Estadieu.

pp. 130–34: Hotel rooms. Photos by M. D.

p. 136: Room at the Oberoi Grand, Kolkata. Image taken from the hotel's website, https://www.oberoihotels.com/hotels-in-kolkata/rooms-suites/.

p. 139: "House," Paris. Photo by M. D.

p. 140: Gymnasium, Grande-Synthe, France, 2018. Photo by M. D.

p. 142: "Habitat," between Calais and Dunkerque, France. Photo by M. D.

p. 144 (*top*): Hôtel Terminus, Niamey. Photo by M. D.

p. 144 (*bottom*): Calais cemetery. Photo by M. D.

p. 145: Holiday Inn Hotel, Calais. Photo by M. D.

p. 146: Illustration of street lamps from the *Larousse Universel* encyclopedia (Paris: Librairie Larousse, 1922).

p. 148: Advertisement. Rights reserved.

p. 150: Advertisement. Rights reserved.

p. 151: Screenshot from *Les Shadoks*, a television series created by Jacques Rouxel, Jean-Paul Couturier, and Claude Piéplu, 1968–1973. © by AAA (Animation art graphique audiovisuel).

p. 152: My father. Rights reserved.

p. 154 (*left*): Andreas Vesalius, illustration from *De humani corporis fabrica* (Basel: Johannes Oporinus, 1543).

p. 154 (*right*): World globe. Photo by M. D.

p. 156: Wuhan, March 17, 2018. Photo by M. D.

p. 160 (*top*): Forest in the Andes. Photo by M. D.

p. 160 (*bottom*): A farmed spruce tree. Photo by M. D.

p. 161: Chernobyl Exclusion Zone. Photo by M. D.

p. 163: Gustave Doré, illustration from Dante Alighieri's *La Divine Comédie*, vol. 1, *L'Enfer* (Paris: Hachette, 1862). Image taken from the Bibliothèque nationale de France's digital library, Gallica.

p. 165: Screenshot of Campo Ma'an, Google Earth.

p. 167: Road in Cameroon. Photo by M.D.

p. 168: Hotel room. Photo by M. D.

pp. 173 and 177: Cameroonian forest. Photos by M. D.

p. 178: At the mouth of the Ntem River. Photo by M. D.

p. 181: Awakening in Jordan. Photo by O.R.

p. 182 (*top*): Hitchhiking in Norway. Photo by O.R.

p. 182 (*bottom*): Hitchhiking in Patagonia. Photo by O.R.

p. 183: Certificate of family debts. Photo by M. D.

p. 185 (*top and bottom*): Argentine beaches. Photos by M. D.

p. 186: Sketch of uterus. Photo by M. D.

p. 187: Incubator. Photo by M. D.

p. 190: Nelly Blumenthal, *Famille de suricates* (Meerkat family). © by Nelly Blumenthal.

p. 191: Fabrice Hyber, *Cerveau rapide* (Quick brain), 2010. © 2021 by ADAGP, Paris.

p. 192: Manuscript page. Photo by M. D.

p. 194: Bath time. Image taken from "32 Photos of Young Housewives from Between the 1940s and 1950s," *Vintage Everyday* (blog), December 17, 2016, https://www.vintag.es/2016/12/vintage-housewives-32-lovely-vintage.html.

p. 197: Mending supplies. Photo by M. D.

pp. 199–200: Polysomnographic examination. Photos by M. D.

p. 201: Sleep curves. Rights reserved.

p. 203: Illustration of a locomotive from the *Nouveau petit Larousse illustré* (Paris: Larousse, 1924).

p. 206: Illustrations of a transorbital lobotomy from A. M. Fiamberti's article "Technique et indications de la leucotomie transorbitaire" (1948). Image taken from Michel Caire's website Histoire de la psychiatrie en Franc, http://psychiatrie.histoire.free.fr/traitmt/lobo.htm.

p. 211: Adão Iturrusgarai, *Portrait de l'autrice en insomniaque* (Portrait of the author as an insomniac). © by Adão Iturrusgarai.

p. 213: Plane to Kinshasa. Photo by M. D.

p. 219: Rwandan Lake. Photo by M. D.

p. 220: The Bisesero Genocide Memorial. Photo by M. D.

p. 222: Lydie Arickx, *Insomnuit* (Insomnight). © by Lydie Arickx. Photo by Alex Bianchi.

p. 224: Europa Ferris wheel, Dresden. Photo by M. D.

p. 225: Screenshot from *Un Chien Andalou* (An Andalusian dog), a twenty-one-minute short film written by Luis Buñuel and Salvador Dalí, directed by Buñuel with cinematography by Albert Duverger.

p. 228: Lake Kivu, Rwanda. Photo by M. D.

p. 229: Rwandan forest. Photo by M. D.

p. 230: Gorillas in Rwanda. Photo by M. D.

p. 234: Illustration of a pangolin from Georges-Louis Leclerc's *Œuvres complètes de Buffon*, vol. 9 (1884–86). Image taken from the Bibliothèque nationale de France's digital library, Gallica.

p. 237: Illustration of an axolotl from *Popular Science Monthly*, vol. 20, November 1881–April 1882.

p. 238: Stuffed animal, Chernobyl Exclusion Zone. Photo by M. D.

p. 239: White rhinos, Hlane National Park, Eswatini. Photo by M. D.

p. 241: Thylacines, etching from 1883. Rights reserved.

p. 242: Old growth rainforest, Tasmania. Photo by M. D.

p. 243: Last known photo of a thylacine, Hobart Zoo, Tasmania, 1933. Photo by Harry Burrell. G. P. Whitley Papers, Australian Museum Archives, Sydney.

p. 244: Dodo skeleton, Natural History Museum, London.

pp. 246–47: Sleeping Odette. Photos by M. D.

p. 249: Greyhound with eyes half-closed, Royal Monastery of Brou, Burgundy. Photo © by Nelly Blumenthal.

p. 251: Pripyat, Chernobyl Exclusion Zone. Photo by M. D.

p. 252: "Negative hands," Caves of Gargas, Hautes-Pyrénées, France. Rights reserved.

p. 253: Moon. Photo by M. D.

p. 254: Henri Rousseau, *Le Rêve* (The dream), 1910. Oil on canvas, 204.5 × 299 cm. Museum of Modern Art, New York.